FADING LIGHT

GW01463892

Jordan and Sophie

Note for Librarians: A cataloguing record for this book is available from Library and Archives Canada at www.collectionscanada.ca/amicus/index-e.html
ISBN 1-4120-7599-8

Printed in Victoria, BC, Canada. Printed on paper with minimum 30% recycled fibre. Trafford's print shop runs on "green energy" from solar, wind and other environmentally-friendly power sources.

TRAFFORD
PUBLISHING™
Offices in Canada, USA, Ireland and UK
This book was published *on-demand* in cooperation with Trafford Publishing. On-demand publishing is a unique process and service of making a book available for retail sale to the public taking advantage of on-demand manufacturing and Internet marketing. On-demand publishing includes promotions, retail sales, manufacturing, order fulfilment, accounting and collecting royalties on behalf of the author.

Book sales for North America and international:
Trafford Publishing, 6E–2333 Government St.,
Victoria, BC v8t 4p4 CANADA
phone 250 383 6864 (toll-free 1 888 232 4444)
fax 250 383 6804; email to orders@trafford.com
Book sales in Europe:
Trafford Publishing (uk) Limited, 9 Park End Street, 2nd Floor
Oxford, UK ox1 1hh UNITED KINGDOM
phone 44 (0)1865 722 113 (local rate 0845 230 9601)
facsimile 44 (0)1865 722 868; info.uk@trafford.com
Order online at:
trafford.com/05-2494

10 9 8 7 6 5 4 3

FADING LIGHT

CHAPTER ONE

The realisation that I had done something wrong hit me before I had made it halfway down the stairs. How I thought that killing Tom would in any way put things right was just a misconception of the frail state of my fucked up mind. I had felt so confident that doing away with him would rid everybody of their pain that I hadn't stopped to think that I was just making things worse.

The screams and shouts I could hear from the scene I had left behind brought me closer to any sort of reality than I had been at any time over the past few weeks and I almost tripped down the last few steps such was my rush to get away. Even when I pushed through the door of Mulvey's club and made it outside I could still hear the cries of Dean echoing through my head.

What the fuck have I done?

I kept repeating the same words over and over again.

What the fuck have I done?

I jumped nervously as the door behind me banged shut and I turned around to face it half expecting Dean and Mikey to come rushing out but thankfully no one was there.

It had been less than a minute since I had plunged the knife into Tom's chest yet I was already in a state of paranoia. How could I think that they would have had time to get dressed? I had to get away fast just in case they did. Maybe Mikey wouldn't be angry with me but Dean definitely would, after all I had just murdered his father. He may have been a cruel bastard to Dean but he was still family.

I couldn't afford to hang around so took off quickly without any thought to where I was headed, I was sure Dean would have called the police almost immediately and because of that I needed as much distance between myself and the club as I could get. The place would soon be a hive of activity and I needed time to think, to try to come to terms with what I had just done. I ran down to the end of the road and turned the corner towards the pub that Mary worked in. I could have done with a few scotches to help clear my head but there was no way that I was going inside. I wasn't even sure if it was open.

I had no idea what time it was.

I carried on running, straight past the pub and down another couple of side streets before I slowed into a walk all the time looking around to make sure I wasn't being followed. I was convinced that the few people I had nearly collided with in my haste to get away knew what I had done. All eyes seemed to be on me but I must have looked a bit odd acting the way I was, stupidly attracting attention to myself. It wasn't what I wanted, I needed to be inconspicuous, I needed to go unnoticed.

I stopped briefly to look at myself, checking for any blood that may have splattered onto my clothes. I couldn't see any marks and I guessed I had what Tom was wearing to thank for that.

Shit, what the fuck had I done?

The words came back into my head and I knew I couldn't stand still a moment longer. I hadn't a clue where I was and I needed to start making definite decisions about where I was going. My first thought was to go back to Dad's but that idea was instantly rebuffed as it was the first place the police would come looking for me. I thought of Mary again; I had said that I would sort it for her and in that respect I had even though I had done it in a way that she definitely would not have agreed with. I couldn't go there, I didn't know where she lived for one thing and what if Mikey came back, what would happen then? How would he react knowing what he knew? How would he even react to his own mother? He was going to be one fucked up little boy and that was my fault.

My pace quickened as I thought and I wasn't taking much notice of how many corners I turned, how many roads I crossed, I was just walking aimlessly until I'd made a definite plan. A car horn sounded as I stepped off a kerb and I looked up at the driver gesticulating at my lack of attention. I smiled meekly back at him as an offer of apology and as I did so noticed about a hundred yards in front of me, the train station.

I knew instantly what I was going to do. I was going to go back to my own home. It would give me time to think, to collect my thoughts and to plan the next few days.

I checked my pockets for some money and pulled out a few notes hoping that it would be enough for the fare. I hurried into the station ticket office and checked the timetable before asking the clerk for a single ticket on the next train home.

It wasn't due to depart for nearly an hour so I disappeared into the waiting room where I started to get a feeling of déjà vu, a trip back to when I left home as a teenager. I was running away again only this time I knew it wouldn't be for long...I was wanted for murder.

FADING LIGHT

CHAPTER TWO

The journey itself was a nightmare. I couldn't concentrate for any longer than a minute on what I wanted to do. I couldn't take stock of the situation I had created for so many reasons and every slight noise distracted me to the point of panic. I kept watch on both entrances to the carriage convinced that every time we stopped en route the police would board the train with the sole intention of arresting me. I told myself it wasn't possible, that they couldn't know where I was but it didn't reassure me. They were professionals, if they knew who I was then it was plausible that they could work out where I was heading. I was tempted to leave the train, to disappear onto a crowded platform and take my chance in a town I wasn't familiar with.

I dismissed the idea as pointless, I didn't have any money so there was no chance of finding anywhere to stay or even getting a bite to eat. I had no choice; I had to go home.

It was dark when I reached my station and it was only when I made it through the exit that I realised I had a long walk ahead of me. Almost three miles and I wasn't in the mood for it. I was desperate for familiar surroundings and somewhere I could shut the door on everything albeit only temporarily.

A few cars passed as I started my trek and I hopefully stuck out my thumb to try and cadge a lift, no one stopped and after twenty minutes I gave up trying resigned to the fact that nobody would.

I cursed as I felt the beginnings of rain, shivering at the feelings of coldness that accompanied it. I started to hurry as the few spots turned into a heavy shower giving me unwanted visions of the night of my sixteenth birthday.

I cursed again.

It seemed that everything had turned full circle but this time I only had myself to blame. In my quest to put everything right I had only made things a million times worse for myself.

They were thoughts I had to get out of my head as quickly as possible and I was thankful that the rain seemed to ease. I was wet through but began to imagine myself relaxing in a steaming hot bath and it was the thought of that which made me hurry further still.

The more familiar I got with the surroundings the happier I began to feel and it wasn't long before I was getting my keys out to open my front door.

FADING LIGHT

It was cold and uninviting when I first entered but putting on the lights made a huge difference. I went upstairs and flicked the switch to the immersion hoping it wouldn't take too long for the water to heat so I could have the bath I'd been dreaming about.

I was desperate for a drink and once downstairs I opened the door of the cocktail cabinet grabbing one of the many bottles of scotch. Not bothering with etiquette I drank straight from the bottle. It was good, an instant warmth that I greatly needed. Still clutching the bottle I shut the curtains in an attempt to block out my lights from the outside world, I was glad to be home but didn't want anyone to know I was there. I took another swig from the bottle and collapsed into my armchair. The bath could wait, I was going to blank everything out with whisky.

I must have dozed off almost at once and it was the sudden ringing of the telephone that made me jump up out of my chair. The bottle fell from my lap onto the floor and I quickly made a grab for it to stop the precious liquid being wasted. I drank again from the rescued bottle and stood still waiting for whoever was calling to give up. I wasn't going to answer.

I looked at the bottle and strangely, as it was almost empty, I didn't feel at all affected. I hadn't wasted much on the floor so why wasn't I a little bit pissed? I caught sight of the clock on the wall above the fireplace, seven thirty it read. For a moment I thought it had stopped whilst I had been away but then I heard it ticking steadily. I went over to the window and pulled the curtains open a fraction.

It was seven thirty in the morning.

The heavy curtains and the front room light still being on had distorted the fact that it was the start of another day. I felt slightly disorientated and uncomfortable, I'd been asleep longer than I'd imagined and it was as though I'd lost a few hours of my life. I suddenly felt cold and realised that my clothes were still damp from the previous nights rain.

I desperately needed that bath.

Putting the bottle down carefully on the coffee table I disappeared upstairs to the bathroom not returning until I'd bathed and put on clean clothes.

Once downstairs my attention again focused on the scotch but this time I took it into the kitchen and poured myself a glassful. I drank it purposefully and opened the fridge door as I did so. I was hungry but the smell that greeted me almost turned my stomach. Something had gone off...badly. I didn't stop to find out what it was, just slammed the door shut.

I needed food so I had to go out and get some. The corner shop a couple of streets away would have to do even though I thought I was taking a big risk. I couldn't be sure if news of what I had done had reached the daily papers. If it had and I was recognised then it wouldn't be long before the police would be sniffing about.

I was there and back in less than ten minutes. Luckily for me I didn't see anyone except the shop assistant. I grabbed a loaf of bread and a pint of milk and just for my own curiosity a couple of papers. There was nothing on the front covers so I hoped what I'd done had been too late to make the printing deadlines. I still had to check the inside pages just to make sure but was confident I had at least the rest of the day to plan my next move.

I flicked through the papers whilst putting a couple of slices of bread in the toaster. I pulled out a jar of marmalade from the cupboard and braved the fridge again in search of the butter. There was nothing in either paper about my crime and I smiled, not that I had anything to smile about…it was only a matter of time.

CHAPTER THREE

I finished my toast in the kitchen before heading back into the front room. It was quite dark in there because of the drawn curtains but still light enough to move around easily. I was pretty sure that none of my neighbours had noticed I was back and felt heartened by that fact. Although we were friendly towards one another I knew I couldn't face anyone knocking at my door. Most of them knew my reasons for going back to see my dying mother but I hadn't been in contact with any of them since I'd been away and it wasn't the time to start.

I began to think of Dad and what he must be going through; Mum had just died and I had disappeared without a word. I wondered if he already knew what I had done and I was tempted to call him. Maybe it had been him that had tried calling earlier that morning.

I decided against it. I was convinced that the police had already been round and were keeping watch on the place after finding out I wasn't there. I remembered reading once that criminals very often returned to the scene of their crime, some sort of morbid fascination with what they had done and guessed that the police would be hoping that I would do just that.

Maybe I would return; I needed to know what was going on. There was so much uncertainty in my mind that I was almost in a state of suspense, not to the degree of excitement more of a tense anxiousness. I needed to talk to someone who knew me and knew what was happening.

Mulvey.

Somehow I had to get in touch with him, but how? He had gone away after Sami's accident and not let anyone know where he was going.

Damn!

It was more or less my idea for him to go and now when I needed him he wasn't there. I tried to think how long he had been away, I seemed to remember that it was only going to be for a few days but circumstances in my own life had made me lose all track of time. Had he only just gone or was he due back any time? I made up my mind to call the club in the hope that he had already returned; maybe just maybe he had heard about the murder and had rushed back to find out more. I slumped down into my armchair just as I had done the previous night and sighed, I had made one positive decision but that wasn't enough.

I looked towards the clock to find out the time but

my eyes were instead drawn towards the mantelpiece and in particular a picture on it...a young girl smiling...a beautiful memory of the past.

Alice.

It was the only picture I had and I was so glad that I had taken it during the precious few months we had been together. I felt a lump in my throat. Alice...someone else who wasn't around when I needed them.

I swallowed hard; I needed to keep positive, I couldn't let myself fall back on sentiment. She wasn't alive and she couldn't help me. I began to feel that she was in a better place. Maybe that was the answer; maybe killing myself would put an end to my problems. I'd thought about suicide once before and that was at a time when my life had really hit rock bottom, I hadn't carried it out then and there was no way I was going to do it now.

I diverted my gaze away from Alice's photo and up towards the clock, it was approaching ten. The day was running away from me, I needed to call Mulvey as soon as possible.

Luckily for me I could recall the number of the club, it was only four digits and as I knew the area code for Mum and Dad having called many times before, I quickly dialled the number.

It rang and rang.

Nobody answered.

Even though it was too early in the day for the club to be open I had hoped that somebody would be there if only because they were tidying up the mess I'd left behind. I didn't even think that it might have been cordoned off as a crime scene and it didn't occur to me that if anyone did pick up the phone it would more than likely be someone from the police force.

Six or seven times over the next two hours I tried the number each time getting the same negative response. I was becoming agitated about the whole situation, the hours were ticking away and I couldn't help feeling that soon the police would be closing their net. I needed to be one step ahead of them so I had to start thinking as though I was one of them. I tried to determine what they could possibly know and what they may have done in their efforts to apprehend me. Obviously they knew who they were looking for; Dean and Mikey would have let them know. Wouldn't they? Suddenly I wasn't sure they knew who I was, I knew who they both were but that was through Mary and Jessie. I had only spoken briefly to Mikey on the phone to arrange for him to be at the club but I couldn't recall Dean being aware of who I was. I was being ridiculous, it wouldn't take too much detective work to find out. Half an hour at the most...I was running Mulvey's club in his absence, shit I'd forgotten I had even performed there. Dean and Jessie had been in the audience watching. Everyone knew who I was so who was I to think that I could get away with it. The brief hope that I could, disappeared. There was no way on this earth that I could be described as a mystery killer. I could imagine that the evening papers were all busy planning their headlines along the lines of... Entertainer sought after club murder...

It was time to be logical. The police had a name, they would know I had been living at Dad's house and they would know where my own house was...they were bound to be on their way.

It was that one thought that made me recognise that up until then I had been lucky but once more I had to get away from where I was. I mulled over an idea, if they were coming my way then why shouldn't I do the opposite and go back from where I had just come.

CHAPTER FOUR

I spent the next ten minutes rushing around collecting together a few bits and pieces for what I predicted would be a long night ahead and it was just after one when I left home with the small backpack slung over my shoulder. I'd purposely taken the picture of Alice from its place on the mantelpiece because if anything happened and I was caught then the thought of not seeing her face again would have been too much to bear.

I planned to catch the train again but one that wouldn't get me back until it was quite late hoping that it would be easier for me to go unnoticed if it was dark. I had a few hours to kill, the unexpected pun bringing a much-needed smile to my otherwise grim expression, so decided to walk the couple of miles to the seafront taking care to keep my head bowed as I passed the many people who were out and about. A few deckchairs were scattered along the prom and I chose to sit in one that was far enough away from the seaside attractions that were on display. For once I felt quite safe.

I stared out across the sea remembering that this

was the one place in the world that I had ever felt happy with my life. I began thinking of Mum. I hadn't even had time to grieve. I wasn't blaming her but I couldn't help feeling that if only she hadn't got ill then none of my current woes would ever have happened. Everything had been perfect until then. Sure I would have still hated Tom, that feeling would never have gone away but at least he couldn't harm me thanks to the distance I'd put between us.

It was a reasonably warm day and that was something I was certainly appreciative of. It meant I could stay where I was for as long as necessary without having to rush off for shelter from the elements.

I began to doubt whether I was doing the right thing in choosing to return. Perhaps it would be better for me to disappear completely, start another new life in another town or maybe another country. That would have proved difficult though as I had never been abroad before and never had the need for a passport and getting one would probably be impossible as I assumed my picture was going to be splashed all over the newspapers and quite possibly the television screens. Damn, I wished I knew what was going on, I couldn't stand the uncertainty of not knowing. I toyed with the idea of buying an evening paper but felt that it would be a little more sensible if I waited until I got to the station. I was a local, and a celebrity at that, and more likely than not I was going to be the main topic of conversation for a few days. The place would be buzzing with rumour and it would be best not to show my face in any of the local shops. I knew I would be better off if I tried to mingle with the day trip tourists as they prepared to return to their respective destinations recognising that it would be easier not to be noticed if I was in a large crowd.

Time passed quite slowly and I tried to form a plan of action for when I finally made it back. I couldn't rule out the possibility that the police were still keeping a watch on his house and that was one of the reasons that I had decided to delay my return until nightfall. I knew my estate like the back of my hand and I didn't think that getting into my childhood home would cause me any great problem. I would probably frighten the life out of my father and I wished I could contact him to let him know what I intended to do but that might have proved to be careless. I didn't know how seriously the police would be treating the case and wasn't sure if they would be monitoring the phone line. Maybe I was over reacting, surely a murder inquiry wouldn't warrant that sort of attention to detail, kidnap and subsequent ransom demands possibly but for my crime I doubted it. They had no need to resort to tactics like that...I was a well-known personality and was bound to be caught sooner rather than later...an ordinary member of the public was more than likely to let them know of my whereabouts.

At around six thirty I left the promenade and headed off to the station. It was about half a mile from where I had been sat and I estimated it would take about twenty minutes to get there. The ticket office was crowded when I went in and the clerk behind the desk looked stressed, he was in the middle of an argument with an irate customer about delayed trains. In a strange way I felt quite pleased as it meant he would probably be surly to every other customer he dealt with afterwards and therefore less likely to look me in the eyes reducing the chances of me being recognised. When it came to my turn I was right, he was in such a bad mood following his previous argument that he dealt with my request quite rudely.

I left the counter and made my way to the newspaper stand still keeping my head bowed as best I could. I was about fifteen feet away when I saw what I wasn't hoping to see. The evening paper was on display with a huge headline... WANTED...and a picture of me. I stopped in my tracks and stared. My heartbeat, which up until that moment had been relatively calm, doubled in its rate. I felt cold as all the blood seemed to drain from my face and I started to shake. It was that moment more than any that made what I had done become real. As much as I wanted to I couldn't bring myself to buy the paper. How could I hand over my money to the assistant when my face was staring back at her? I turned and ran towards the platform that my train was due to depart from hoping that it had arrived early and I could disappear into a carriage away from everyone.

It wasn't there but thankfully I didn't have to wait long. There were quite a few empty compartments and I got into one slamming the door shut behind me. I sat in the seat closest to the window and just stared out. If anyone else entered there was no way that I was going to speak to them. I clutched my backpack close to my chest, a million thoughts reverberating around my mind. I was still shaking and I was convinced that I was making a huge mistake in going back but I knew I had to, there was too much I had to sort out. I briefly thought about giving myself up, that it wasn't going to be worth the mental stress of the next few hours, however I had no choice but to keep going...I had people to talk to before I lost my freedom. What chance would I have to explain to Dad from a prison cell?

I was hungry and rummaged through my belongings searching for the cheese sandwich I'd hastily made before I left home triumphantly bringing it out to eat. The picture of Alice was smiling out of the bag at me and I looked back at it before taking it out so that I could see it more clearly. I remembered the few words Tom said to me before I plunged the knife into him.

She was coming to find me.

She had finally plucked up enough courage to tell him about us and she wanted to find me. I'd been in such a panic I hadn't stopped to think just what those few words meant but now in my isolated state I could reflect.

The train jerked into life and slowly pulled out of the station. It was starting to get dark outside but not as dark as my world felt to me.

Why did she have to tell him?

Why couldn't she have just walked out?

In a way I was proud of her because telling him about me would have really hurt him but it wasn't worth risking her life for. I tried to imagine what those last few moments had been like for her, had she called out for me as she fell down the stairs? Maybe Jessie knew, maybe if I ever saw her again I could ask her.

The train continued on its journey, nobody got into my carriage and the dilemma of not talking to anyone didn't materialise. The more I thought of Alice the calmer I became; it was as though she was there with me. My earlier thoughts of her not being there for me when I needed her vanished, her life must have been hell. Two people so miserable apart who could have been so happy together. She loved me until the end.

A few tears dropped from my eyes and I was certain that if Alice had been able to deal with her life the way she obviously had then I could do the same...It didn't matter if I was caught.

CHAPTER FIVE

It was one o'clock in the morning and I was sat in the playground opposite the George, a place where so much had happened that in one way or another had influenced the direction of my life. I was so close to home yet I was too terrified to walk the final few streets. I felt like I was about to close the last chapter of my life, a life that for me would now be meaningless, trapped for the rest of it in a tiny prison cell.

I'd been there for about an hour gathering my thoughts, contemplating my next move and was beginning to think that it was too late to be bothering Dad. I was all too aware that I would probably frighten the life out of him when I finally entered the house, voices in my head were telling me that there wasn't any point, that I should just leave him alone. How long had it been since Mum died? Three or four days? I couldn't remember, time had become irrelevant, every minute to me seemed like hours.

I couldn't leave him alone though could I?

We needed to talk to each other and I didn't know if I was likely to get another chance.

FADING LIGHT

That was it...the time had come.

Dad was the closest person to me and if I couldn't explain things to him then I wouldn't be able to talk to anyone. I got up from the bench and slowly made my way towards the house feeling a little nervous when I reached the end of his road; the anticipation that something was about to happen was at the forefront of my mind. Slowly I edged my way down the street keeping in the shadows as best I could. There were one or two cars parked on either side of the road, none were obviously police cars but I didn't expect them to be. I tried to peer through the darkness in an effort to make out shapes that might be sitting in the front seats but my vision wasn't clear enough. A car door slammed in the distance and I ducked into a driveway my heart thumping wildly. They must have been waiting and spotted me...now it was all over, my brief time on the run had come to an end. I stayed where I was, crouched down amongst the bushes, for about ten minutes. Nothing happened, no one approached, no police...nobody. I breathed a huge sigh of relief and stood up. I was trembling and didn't feel I could go any further but I was so close I had to. I was unwilling to finish my journey along the pavement so for the last hundred yards or so I went through the neighbours' gardens. Only one dividing hedge proved difficult but I eventually managed to push myself through it without making too much noise. Finally I made it and I felt the tension in my body diminish as I opened and then closed the door behind me.

"Who's there?" came the shout almost immediately. The front room door burst open and Dad came rushing out, arm raised as if ready to strike.

"Dad!" I shouted back, instinctively raising my own arms to protect myself.

The blow wasn't forthcoming as Dad recognised my voice.

"What the hell are you doing? You frightened the life out of me. I thought they were back again"

It wasn't quite the arrival I had been expecting. It was nearly two in the morning and I had anticipated that the house would be quiet and that Dad would be in bed. Why was he up and why was he so agitated? What did he mean by saying 'I thought they were back?'

Something crunched under my feet as I followed him back into the front room. I was about to ask him what he meant when he flung open the curtains; I was shocked by what I saw. One of the front windows was boarded up and there was glass all over the sill, I realised just what I had been stepping on. It was everywhere.

"What happened?" I asked.

Dad didn't answer the question I posed, instead he picked up a newspaper and flung it at me angrily.

"What the fuck have you done?"

I knew what he meant and it was my turn not to answer. I picked up the scattered paper and began reading, somehow I had hoped that Dad wouldn't have known but seeing it written in black and white I knew I would be in for a tough time. Parents expect and want the best for their children and I had let him down in the most horrific way possible. I couldn't imagine the humiliation I must have caused him. This had come at what was already the worst time of his life.

I read on past the WANTED headline; something wasn't quite right. The story wasn't reading the way I thought it would. Tom was in intensive care, critical but not dead. I hadn't killed him; he was still alive.

For some reason I burst out laughing, I couldn't believe it; I felt like celebrating.

"He's not dead!" I shouted, looking towards Dad who was quite rightly astounded by my reaction.

"It's not funny Roo," he bellowed "you tried to kill someone."

It brought me back to my senses. Dad was right and I thought I had, I'd plunged the knife deep into his chest, I'd seen the blood and he was gasping for breath...he had to be dead. Was the story made up? Were the police trying to flush me out of hiding by giving me the idea that I hadn't killed him? The exhilaration I had felt quickly evaporated, it was still real. Whatever the outcome it was still at the very least attempted murder. It was still a crime.

I needed a drink.

I remembered storing a bottle where I knew Dad wouldn't find it. Although I was a grown man I knew his views on alcohol hadn't changed but at that moment in time it didn't matter.

When I returned from fetching it Dad was sitting in his armchair, he looked terrible. Whether it was because of Mum dying or what I had done I didn't want to know.

He looked up at me.

"What in God's name possessed you?" he asked me.

"You don't want to know." I replied taking a swig from the bottle.

"Yes I do, I want to know everything. I want to understand. You don't do things like that without a reason."

Dad was speaking quietly and I could tell how

upset he was. How could I let him know my reasons for trying to kill Tom? It wasn't just my secret...there were other people involved. Even though it was my revenge I thought I could justify it because of what Tom had done to so many lives. Maybe I could have used their stories as an excuse but how fair would that have been and how would it make me look? I wasn't going to say too much. Dad could keep asking questions but I was going to be as vague as I thought necessary.

"I always knew you'd do time because of that bastard, how many times did I warn you?"
He wasn't entirely right, he had always warned me about Tom getting me into trouble but this was different. It was my choice. Tom didn't tell me to stab him.
I had to tell Dad something. I hadn't seen him since I'd run out of hospital just after Mum had died. He knew I had fallen out with Jessie, that there was some sort of problem between us. Maybe I could somehow concoct a story around that. I didn't think he knew that Jessie was Tom's daughter and I thought that perhaps I should tell him, say that Tom had found out about us and cornered me in the club. In an act of self-defence I stabbed him. It sounded good in theory but I couldn't lie, not to Dad anyway and it wasn't fair on Jessie. No matter how bad I felt about our

relationship none of it was her fault.

"I'm sorry Dad," I started to say, "I can't explain, I have my reasons but..."

My sentence trailed off as something crashed through the remaining window. I was showered with shards of glass as the object narrowly missed the back of my head. Dad was up on his feet instantly and out through the front door before I had chance to comprehend what was happening.

"Dad!" I called out in a vain attempt to stop him. He didn't listen; he was off down the path and into the road shouting at the top of his voice before I had time to move.

"Bastards!" I could hear him saying as I eventually caught up with him. I didn't know what to say. Even though I hadn't seen him I knew it was Dean who had thrown the brick. It was meant for me, there was no doubt about that. Did he know I was there or was he trying to get at me by intimidating Dad? I hoped he hadn't stayed around to see the aftermath of his actions because he would have seen me as I dashed out into the road. I couldn't imagine what he would have done if he had. Anything could have happened and I had to get Dad back in the house as quickly as I could.

I was quite badly cut from the flying glass and Dad tended to my injuries gently. I couldn't help thinking that I wouldn't have been as sympathetic if I had been in his shoes. This was all happening because of me and Dad was taking the brunt of it. He was angry I knew that, but his anger was justified; I had let him down so badly.

"I'm sorry Dad." I said again and went to put my arms around him but he pulled away.

I had a lot of explaining to do.

CHAPTER SIX

We didn't speak to each other much after that. I thought it best we tried again after a few hours sleep. I fixed boards to the broken windows and tidied up as best I could. Dad just sat in his chair watching. I suggested that he went to bed when I'd finished but he said he didn't want to. I shrugged my shoulders and said goodnight but Dad didn't reply.

It was a restless night, my body was tired but my mind was active. I didn't really want to sleep just in case Dean came back intent on inflicting more damage on the house. He wouldn't be able to break any more downstairs windows but I thought it would be quite easy for him to break in. The boards I'd fixed in place were quite flimsy and I made up my mind to fix them properly in the morning. I couldn't risk Dad living like that for too long.

I vowed to try to contact Mulvey as soon as I could. I didn't have to ask him about Tom any more but I still needed to talk to him. I'd been there for him when Sami died so I hoped he'd have some sort of support for me. Obviously he didn't know how involved Tom was in relation to Sami but that was something he didn't need to know, not ever.

Morning came quickly enough and I was up by seven thirty. I'd been in bed less than four hours and I was surprised to see that Dad was already downstairs. I wanted our relationship back on an even keel and I knew it was up to me to try and sort it out; being friendly would be a start.

"Hi Dad," I started saying before pausing hoping to get an instant reply. Dad said nothing so I continued.

"I didn't hear you get up, did you sleep well?"

Dad replied that time but was distinctly frosty.

"I haven't slept since Mum died."

I knew then that it was going to be hard work. I hadn't mentioned Mum since I'd been back, not that I'd had chance too, and I wished that I'd stayed up talking all night but the incident with Dean had put paid to that.

"I can't sleep in that bed any more."

I didn't know what Dad was trying to do, was he trying to make me feel guilty? Did he think I wasn't grieving for Mum? Maybe I wasn't, maybe I was too wrapped up in my own selfish world to really care about any one else.

It wasn't true.

I had thought of Mum, how could he doubt that.

He hadn't seen me, what did he know about anything I had been going through? I was starting to get angry but I had to bite my tongue, I needed Dad's support just as much as he needed mine.

"I miss her too you know." I said as I put both my hands on his shoulders trying to look him directly in the eyes.

He didn't return my gaze but he didn't move away from me, not like he had done the night before. I sighed inwardly as I thought we might just be getting somewhere. I had to be totally on his side regarding Mum.

I waited a few moments until he finally looked back at me.

"The funeral is set for Friday," he said sadly, "I hope you'll be there."

The way he said it was, without doubt, full of sarcasm. I knew he meant if I hadn't been arrested, but whether I had been apprehended or not wasn't down to me.

"Of course I'll be there... whatever happens."

I didn't want to continue the conversation in case it deteriorated into an angry exchange. I needed to get away from Dad temporarily. I remembered the windows needed repairing properly and told him I was off out to get some stronger boards until I could arrange for a glazier to fit new glass. He told me not to bother but I didn't listen and headed off towards the precinct and the local hardware store.

I was back within the hour struggling with half a dozen boards and took another hour fixing them into place. I didn't do a particularly professional job but nobody was going to be able to break in.

My next task was to try and get hold of Mulvey and I picked up the phone dialling the number of the club on the off chance that he might have made it back. I was expecting the phone to ring and ring but surprisingly it was picked up almost immediately. I recognised the voice at once.

"It's me, Roo." I answered to his booming greeting.

"Shit Roo, what the fuck have you done?"

I couldn't recall ever hearing Mulvey swear before and they seemed to be the words that were on everybody's lips. Dad and Mulvey had used exactly the same sentence as I had when I was making my escape from the club but they were only echoing my own feelings... what the fuck had I done? Even though I knew I hadn't murdered Tom it was still serious enough.

"I need to talk to you," I blurted out to Mulvey, "I'm coming to the club!"

Mulvey didn't argue even though I expected him to suggest somewhere else to meet. I didn't even ask if it was safe for me to go there; the fact that the police might still be carrying out forensics at the club had gone clean out of my mind.

I left straight away without telling Dad where I was going and walked briskly towards the precinct and the bus stop where I waited for about fifteen minutes before boarding the bus into town. Twenty minutes later I was standing outside the door of Mulvey's club. I felt uneasy as I knocked, I didn't know what to expect when I went inside. I had a graphic mental image of Tom lying on the floor with blood still pumping from his chest, Dean and Mikey with hands covered in the crimson liquid as they tried in vain to stem the flow.

The scene vanished as soon as Mulvey flung open the door and virtually dragged me inside; he looked quickly in both directions then slammed the door shut before turning to face me. He didn't have to say anything because I could see in his expression just how shocked he was.

"I had to do it." I started to explain.

"I can't believe that Roo... Why? Who was he? What was he doing there?"

"I can't tell you, you don't need to know." I began before changing the subject, "Can I have a scotch?"

Mulvey shrugged his shoulders, he was getting exasperated.

"Do what you want Roo, just tell me the truth."
I hurried upstairs to the bar knowing that I no longer wanted to be there. Mulvey wasn't going to be of any help, I couldn't even remember what I expected him to do. Whilst I believed I had actually killed Tom I could have used Mulvey as a source of information but it wasn't murder any more and although I knew I was going to serve a stretch in jail I wasn't as desperate as I had been. In a way I was relieved that I hadn't killed him.
I didn't wait for Mulvey to pour me a drink instead I went straight behind the bar and helped myself downing the glassful in seconds. I spotted the door that led to the office and was tempted to check it out. It was true; criminals do have a morbid fascination to revisit the scene of their crime. What was it? Smug self-satisfaction? I didn't look, I didn't have to. I knew it was real...it was all too fresh in my memory.
Mulvey joined me behind the bar and poured himself a drink. He wanted to talk but I didn't. I began to think of Jessie, she was one of the reasons I couldn't tell Mulvey anything. He didn't know who Tom was and what affect he was having on his life in regard to Sami. It was something he was going to find out sometime, the mess I'd made of everything ensured that, but he wasn't going to find out from me. I knew too much and if

he ever found out I couldn't be sure how he was going to react not only towards me but to Jessie as well. She had to be protected.

CHAPTER SEVEN

I didn't stay at the club for long. I had another couple of scotches and listened as Mulvey begged me to give myself up. I told him I couldn't, there was still too much at stake.

I took a bus ride home hoping that Dad had had a chance to come to terms with his anger and would be in a better frame of mind to talk. We needed to because I wanted him on my side for me to be able to face the next few days.

I was feeling quite low, I didn't know why I'd bothered going to see Mulvey and his suggesting that I should give myself up was something I didn't want to hear. Had I told him to do that after Sami's accident when he had more or less forced her off the road?

I put thoughts of Mulvey out of my head as I walked the last few hundred yards. I stopped at the garden gate and looked at the windows. They looked so much worse from the outside and I silently prayed that for Dad's sake everything would soon return to normal.

"I phoned the police while you were out."

Dad's first words to me when I got inside shook

me rigid. I automatically assumed he meant he had turned me in and my first instinct was to run away again.

"I told them about the broken windows."

"And about me?"

"No I never mentioned you. They sent someone round straight away when they realised it was my house that had been attacked but they didn't stay long."

"Do they know I'm here?"

I was getting desperate again even though Dad had told me he hadn't turned me in, I needed him to confirm again that I was still a free man.

"They asked loads of questions about you and if I had heard from you but I said no."

I should have been relieved but to me it just meant that the police would step up patrols around the house. I was only moments away from being caught. How long could I stay? I had to move on but I had nowhere to go. If only Mulvey had been a bit more sympathetic to my situation then I could have gone back there, hidden myself away until I'd sorted out a few things.

"Shit!"

I said it louder than I intended to and was shocked when Dad rounded on me with a venom that I had never witnessed before.

"I want you out of this fucking house!" he

snarled at me, "and I want you to stay out of my fucking life."

I couldn't believe it. He had shouted at me in the past but nothing like that, it was said with so much hatred and barely six inches from my face. I thought for one awful moment that he was going to hit me. How had it got to that level?

"Please Dad," I begged, "don't do this."

"Get the fuck out of my house, I don't ever want to see you again."

I didn't get the opportunity to say anything else as the front door crashed open quickly followed by half a dozen police officers. I had no chance to even think about making an escape as I was pinned up against the wall and handcuffed. I vaguely heard someone mention my name and that I was being arrested on suspicion of attempted murder but it was all a bit of a blur. I looked pleadingly at Dad as if hoping somehow that he could do something to help me but he looked away. Had he lied to me? Had he told them I was there?

"Dad!" I shouted as I was forcibly led up the garden path to a waiting van.

A few neighbours had appeared on the pavement and I glared at them for being so nosy before I was forced into the back of the vehicle and driven away.

I found out later that it was Mulvey who had turned me in. The interrogating officer had let it be known just who my friends were over the next few hours of questioning. I stayed silent for ages as they tried to get me to admit to what I had done but what was the point in me confessing when they already knew I was guilty.

I was allowed to see the duty solicitor so that I could clearly understand the position I was in. I knew I had been arrested but wasn't sure whether or not I'd been formally charged.

He started explaining things to me in legal terms but I was having none of that and told him to tell me straight. I just wanted to know what would happen next and whether I could get out of there.

He waited for me to calm down and then tried to explain as simply as he possibly could. He said that the crime I had been arrested for was a serious and violent one and therefore an indictable offence that would have to go to Crown Court. If I were charged in the near future then I would have to attend a Magistrates Court first usually the following morning, they would then transfer the case for trial in the Crown Court. It was up to the magistrate to decide whether I would be remanded in custody or released on bail until the trial began. He explained that everyone had the right to bail but that as the crime was attempted murder then it was likely that I would be refused. However because of who I was and the likelihood that I wouldn't commit any more offences or abscond it was just possible that I might still be freed on bail.

That's all I wanted to know, I had a chance of getting out albeit for only a couple of months but it was a chance I had to have.

"Sort it for me." I begged. "Please."

The solicitor promised to do his best and I was subsequently charged with attempted murder.

The cell I was taken to stank of sick and urine and I heaved as the smell ripped at the back of my throat. I didn't sleep all night, just sat on the edge of the bed staring at the heavy metal door. A few times the shutter slid open and I could just about make out eyes looking at me. I was starving and thirsty but wasn't offered any food or water. My mood was getting worse by the minute and I didn't think I would be able to keep my mouth shut when I was finally released from the filthy rat hole they had shut me up in. I lost my temper just the once at about three in the morning kicking the bucket they had left for me to piss in around the dingy cell. I made enough noise to wake the dead but nobody took any notice. It was pointless and I probably wasn't doing myself any favours.

Eventually at eight the cell door opened and a

constable came in with a tray on which was a cup of coffee and a bowl of cereal. He announced that I had an appearance in the Magistrates Court at ten thirty and sarcastically suggested that I should try and smarten myself up before I went. My response to his request wasn't pleasant.

The duty solicitor arrived at nine thirty and boosted my spirits by saying that he thought I had a good chance of getting bail.

He was right.

Somehow I was allowed bail but with conditions. I had to reside at Dad's house under strict curfew until my appearance at Crown Court.

CHAPTER EIGHT

Dad was hugely disappointed that I had been ordered to stay at his house whilst awaiting trial. He made a big issue about how he was only letting it happen because I was his son but that he meant what he had said in wanting me out of his life for good. I listened to everything he said agreeing with him when I had to. I couldn't afford another argument with him or I would be back in a police cell quicker than I wanted.

Dean had been back the night I was in custody and sprayed graffiti all over the outside of the house. It made unpleasant reading and I was glad that Mum was no longer alive to witness it. Dad was distraught about it and the attempts he was making to wash it off weren't helping. I wasn't allowed outside the front door so all I could do was watch him get more frustrated and angry by the minute. I tried to calm him down but my efforts were wasted, all I seemed to be doing was making his mood worse.

I noticed a steady stream of people, some of whom had been family friends for years, walking past our house having a good look but not one of them stopped to offer any help.

Dad's frustrations were having an effect on my own mental state. I could relate to a lot of what he was going through because of what had happened in my life over the previous few weeks, maybe it was even worse for him having lost Mum. I remembered promising her that I would look after him when she died but I'd let her down. How could I make sure he was all right from inside a prison cell?

I was sliding once again into depression something I seemed to have had to deal with all of my adult life. I had things I wanted to do, people I wanted to talk to and try to explain why I'd tried to kill Tom. I desperately needed someone who would understand.

It was two days later that I had a visitor. I had been sitting alone in the front room getting more and more pent up. Dad was in the house but he refused to even acknowledge my existence, he wouldn't even offer me any food or eat anything I prepared for him. I told him many times that it was a stupid situation but he wouldn't listen. I didn't think I could stand it for much longer.

I opened the front door and all my old emotions raced through my body as I saw Jessie standing there. I hadn't seen her since I'd pushed her away from me outside the hospital chapel.

"Hi." she said nervously, shifting her gaze down towards her feet.

I didn't know what to say, I wasn't expecting her to turn up at the house and wasn't sure it was a good idea either. Feelings got the better of me though and I greeted her warmly. No matter what I thought of our relationship and whether it could ever continue she was a friendly face and just what I needed. I invited her inside, it wasn't worth the bother of asking Dad if I could but at the same time I knew he wouldn't refuse. He had got on well with Jessie the couple of times they had met and in some way she had been there for him more than I had when Mum had died. The generous gesture of bringing flowers to the chapel would probably have meant more to Dad than anything I had done. I hadn't thought about the aftermath of my attitude when I stormed out of hospital intent on revenge but I was sure that Jessie and Dad had comforted each other, even tidying up the chairs that I had strewn around the corridor in my anger.

Dad appeared from the kitchen to see who had knocked on the door and smiled amiably when he recognised Jessie. They exchanged greetings and Jessie kissed Dad lightly on the cheek. I felt a pang of jealousy, not that I thought Dad fancied her but rather I wished he would show me some of the same affection. I walked into the front room leaving Jessie alone with Dad for a few moments, I didn't want it to seem like I was dragging her away from him. I wanted Dad's good mood to continue for as long as possible.

Soon enough Jessie joined me, smiling broadly as she made her way across the carpet.

"How is he?" she asked.

"That's the first time I've seen him smile. It's a difficult time for him." I replied almost apologetically, I could hardly tell her the truth that we weren't on speaking terms, that I hadn't got a clue how he felt.

"Why are you here?"

I posed the question looking deep into her eyes. She stayed silent for a while before moving away from me to sit in one of the armchairs. Her smile vanished from her face and she looked towards the boarded up windows.

"Is that what he did?"

I hadn't expected a question back from her and for a second wondered what on earth she was talking about. I had briefly forgotten Dean was her brother. I followed her gaze to look at the reason for her question and answered.

"Yes, how did you know?"

"We live in the same house."

Jessie was almost nonchalant in her reply and I

felt a bit stupid; she was bound to know.

"Dean has turned into my Dad these past few days, I've never known him to be so aggressive. He told me he was coming to get you but I didn't think he meant it."

"Do you know what happened at the club?"
Another of my stupid questions, Jessie gave me a look of exasperation.

"Of course I know and I wish you'd fucking killed him!"

"You don't mean that." I said shocked at her outburst.

"Yes I do!" she shouted back at me at which point Dad came rushing into the room. I got the impression he had been listening at the door and he stared at me coldly.

"What's going on?" he demanded fiercely.

"It's o.k. It's nothing."
It was Jessie who replied, not me, as she got out of her seat and stood in front of him as if she was protecting me. Dad made as if to push her aside but Jessie was having none of it.

"It's my fault," she told him "I'm angry at what Dean's been doing."
It took a couple of minutes but then Dad began to calm down. Diplomatically Jessie suggested he make a drink for us and with much reluctance he eventually agreed.

I was relieved and offered my thanks to Jessie but they were shrugged off.

"I shouldn't have shouted." she said before settling back down into the armchair.

"You can't want your own father dead." I carried on the conversation questioning what she had previously said.

"He killed my Mum," she said sadly, "isn't that why you stabbed him? You told me you loved her."

She was right. I had told her that I loved Alice. I'd forgotten about that. I had been so fucked up by so many things I couldn't remember what I'd actually said to Jessie.

"I can't tell you why I stabbed him, you don't need to know."

"Tell me about you and my Mum then?"

Jessie's question was cold and direct but what was I supposed to say to her? I didn't want her to know about my feelings for Alice. I felt like showing her the door but I couldn't, I owed her some sort of explanation.

Dad brought in a tray of tea as I pondered what answer I was going to give her and I waited until he had gone before speaking quietly.

"I did love your mother, but it was a long time ago."

I felt embarrassed telling her, it was like I'd been

having an affair behind her back and I was now confessing my guilt.

"She was seeing Tom, your Dad, at the time. She fell pregnant with Dean and it wasn't mine. I left and moved away. That's all there is to it."

"And you've waited so long to get your revenge? I don't believe you, there's more to it than that."

"Believe what you want, it was the first time I'd seen him since I left, old emotions came flooding back. I didn't set out to kill him."

It was a blatant lie. I'd given her a reason for stabbing Tom it was her choice whether she believed it.

"You should have," she said angrily, "then you would be in prison."

What did she mean by that? Was she beginning to hate me? I didn't want her hatred and I felt like telling her more but I couldn't. There were old wounds that didn't need reopening. Maybe at some point in the future I could tell her everything.

"You'd be safe there," Jessie continued, "Dean wouldn't be able to get you. I love you Roo."

She dashed across the room and flung her arms around me bursting into tears at the same time.

Shit, I thought, I couldn't deal with it. It was time for Jessie to go.

"It's Mum's funeral tomorrow," I said as I gently pushed her away, "will you come?"

CHAPTER NINE

I was quite relieved when Jessie left. She'd agreed to come to Mum's funeral and I managed to convince her that I had things to do in preparation for it. She left smiling and I was glad I had found out that I had at least one friend I could turn to. I still wasn't sure if our relationship could take off again and if I was going to jail for any length of time then it was important that I made a quick decision on what I wanted to do. I was sure that Jessie would put emotional pressure on me and promise to be waiting until I was released and I wouldn't have doubted her loyalty but how old would I be then...forty? It wouldn't be fair on her to wait. I was pretty sure I was going to end it but for the time being I needed her support. I tried talking to Dad but he refused to speak no matter how much I pleaded. It was a hopeless situation and in the end I gave up. I just hoped that a lot of Dad's reluctance was down to the fact that it was the eve of Mum's funeral and he was still trying to deal with his unimaginable loss.

The day dragged on and I found it difficult to deal with the boredom. If only I hadn't been under curfew then at least I would have been able to take a walk somewhere although even that would have probably been a mistake. If Jessie was telling the truth that Dean was out to get me then how was I to know that he wouldn't be lurking behind a corner ready to pounce at the first sight of me?

The hairs on the back of my neck bristled and I had a horrible feeling that he was outside the house that very moment. I rushed upstairs and looked out through my bedroom window but he was nowhere to be seen.

I was getting paranoid. It was still daylight; even Dean wouldn't be foolish enough to blatantly parade himself in front of everybody. He would be back sometime, I had no doubt about that, if Jessie knew where I was then Dean most definitely did as well. I prayed for Dad's sake more than mine that it wouldn't be that night.

FADING LIGHT

CHAPTER TEN

My fears were unwarranted. I awoke early in the morning feeling drained, the previous nights sleep had been disturbed by every slight noise and although I was thankful that Dean hadn't shown up I was still full of trepidation that he might put in an appearance at Mum's funeral at some point. It was a chance for him to either show me that he was around or to actually cause a scene. Even a police presence wouldn't be enough to put him off.

I wasn't looking forward to the day. To my shame Mum had been out of my thoughts due to the events of the past week and now that the day had finally arrived it had, for the first time, begun to hit home that she had actually gone. I shed a few tears privately in my bedroom. For some reason I didn't want Dad to see. I decided to keep out of his way as much as I possibly could; it wasn't a day that he needed me in his face considering the friction that existed between us. I wanted to give him support because I was finally beginning to realise how he must be feeling but I was sure that anything I said no matter how sincere I was trying to be would be thrown back in my face.

I was due to report at the local police station that morning as a condition of my bail but because of the funeral I had been excused. I had been informed that there would be a few officers on duty at the church mainly because of who I was and the attention I had been getting in the press not just on a local basis but nationally as well. I wasn't really aware of how much media interest there was because I hadn't read any newspapers or bothered with the television. I had watched the news on the first night I was back but quite honestly I didn't think anyone was that interested. I just thought it was a personal issue between Tom's family and mine. What concern was it to anybody else?

How wrong I was.

The arrival of the funeral procession at the church was greeted with a total lack of respect by the waiting media. The flashing of cameras and the microphones that were being pushed into my face was shameful to say the least and I for one was thankful the police were there to restrain the pushing crowd.

Dad shot me a glance that to me said he wished I wasn't there. I hadn't expected such a scene and I contemplated taking off but with so many police around I didn't think that would be wise. The press would have a field day if they captured me on film being chased and arrested.

Mum's coffin was unloaded from the hearse and Dad took his place amongst the pallbearers. For a few seconds the waiting journalists went silent and bowed their heads but only until the coffin had disappeared through the church doors. Thankfully they weren't allowed to follow and I entered the relative quiet of the holy building.

I was amazed at how full it was inside guessing there to be at least two hundred people. All the pews were taken and lots more were standing at the back. I knew Mum was popular in the community but surmised that there was a ghoulish aspect surrounding some of those who were there.

Heads turned as we entered, more to look at me than looked at Dad and Mum's coffin, and I knew then that a lot had turned up out of sheer nosiness. What was it? Had they just wanted to get their pictures in the papers or on the television screens? I anticipated a mad scramble when the service was over just for some of the freaks to do that.

I felt a tap on my shoulder just as I turned to walk down the aisle behind the coffin.

It was Jessie.

A massive sense of relief went through my body; I

was so glad that she had turned up. She smiled and I grasped her hand tightly not letting go until we reached the front pew and took our seats. I followed Dad's lead and knelt on one of the cushions to say a brief prayer. All my thoughts were of Mum and I had forgotten about the melee outside that had greeted us. I became oblivious to everything around me and nothing else mattered except the reason I was there.

The doleful tones of the organ changed into something a little more melodic and the congregation rose to sing one of the hymns that Dad had chosen and he sang with gusto as tears streamed down his face. I joined in as best I could but I was choking up inside. Jessie clung to my side sobbing her heart out until the organ stopped playing and we all took our seats again.

The vicar said a few prayers before relating all that was good about my mother to everybody. He knew Mum and Dad personally as they had been church goers for many years although Dad hadn't been at all during Mum's illness. The vicar was really complimentary with the things he said although much of it went over my head. I was quite numb about the whole ordeal and not paying attention to a lot of what he was saying. The hymns and prayers continued along with our ever increasing sadness and it wasn't long before we were following the coffin again only this time out through the side door and into the small cemetery that ran alongside the rear of the church. I spied the plot that had been dug for Mum's coffin already laden with flowers that the true well-wishers had given.

In ten minutes it was all over. Mum had been laid to rest and the graveside congregation began to disperse. Dad, Jessie and I stayed behind for a while for a moment of silence on our own, Jessie with her arms around Dad. I thought that maybe their apparent closeness could be used to bring Dad and I together as father and son again.

A wake had been arranged at the local community hall and in attempt to build bridges with Dad I thought it best that I didn't go. Telling him was hard but he accepted it. I didn't want to have any attention focused on me after what had happened with the press. Dad needed to be around his closest friends so that he could grieve in the right way.

Two police officers were guarding the rear gate to the cemetery and I approached them asking if I could somehow be taken back to Dad's house in one of their cars to try and avoid a repeat of the scenes earlier and after a brief radio conversation with their superiors it was agreed. In a matter of minutes I was rushed to a waiting car and because of the speed of it, it took the press by surprise. Many of them rushed over, flashbulbs exploding in frenzy but it was too late, the car door slammed and I was away. Jessie came with me and I was glad of the company. I had been unsure of what I wanted from her in the future but having had her by my side all morning even allowing for the emotional trauma of it all I knew that we at least had to talk.

Jessie spoke first.

"How are you feeling?" She asked as I slumped down onto the settee.

I patted the cushion next to me beckoning her to join me and she sat down at a slight distance but at an angle so that she could face me.

"I don't know how I feel," I replied dejectedly, "everything is such a mess."

"You know I'm always here for you don't you?" Jessie looked downwards as she spoke and I got the feeling she was expecting rejection. How could I push her away? I wanted her as much as she wanted me.

"Saying that sums up what the problem is." I said reaching out to take one of her hands in mine, "We have to be realistic about everything. I could get ten years in jail. Do you understand how long ten years is?"

"It doesn't matter how long it is. I want you in

my life always."

"You're too young to wait, you need a life, it won't take long for you to forget me."

"Tell me why you did it. If it was for Mum then I can't ever forget you. I lost her from my life too!"

"It wasn't because of your Mum, you don't need to know."

I was saying things that were true but she deserved a proper explanation. I had to give her a believable reason and I had to rack my brains to think of one. I had to devise a way of putting together all the incidents that had affected my ultimate action into a story that could explain everything.

"Please!"

Jessie temporarily interrupted my thoughts. I gazed into her innocent eyes. Maybe that was a way around it; play on her innocence. She was after all young enough to believe anything and I more than anyone would be able to get away with saying whatever I wanted to her.

It came to me suddenly; a flash of memory that connected Tom's life with Mulvey's club...Sami. She could be the reason, she was after all a twenty-four carat bitch and she was dead. Mulvey and Tom didn't know each other so if Mulvey found out then my story would seem plausible. It was going to make me look foolish in front of

Jessie but that didn't matter, her feelings for me were too strong for that to last.

"O.K." I finally said, "but you won't understand that it was me who had to do it. I've thrown a good part of my life away for nothing."

"I want to understand. I need to know what turns someone like you into a killer."

Sometimes Jessie said things that belied her age, maybe she wasn't as naïve as I thought she was. Maybe it was going to be harder than I thought to pull the wool over her eyes. I had to lay it on a bit thick, lie to the point of desperation. It wasn't something that would convince a jury because I was confessing but it was practice for lying if I felt the need to when my case finally came to court.

"You remember telling me about Sami, Samantha, your Dad's girlfriend?"

"What's it got to do with her?" Jessie wanted to know.

"Everything." I replied. "She was Nick's girlfriend, he had just asked her to marry him when she died."

"Who's Nick?"

"Nick...you know, Nick Mulvey...the club owner."

"I don't believe you!"

Jessie stood up letting go of my hand. She faced me with her hands on her hips and she looked angry.

"You're telling me you tried to kill someone because of that? What's it got to do with you? Why couldn't you let them sort it out?"

"I said you wouldn't understand, how could you. You didn't know Nick, you didn't know how fucked up he was."

"That's his problem not yours. He's taken you away from me."

Jessie started crying and ran from the room. I was tempted to go after her but didn't. She needed to come to terms with my actions on her own. It felt bad upsetting her the way I had but at the same time it was good because her reaction meant that she was believing my lies.

Something crashed in the kitchen but it didn't bother me. Jessie had the right to express her anger any way she chose. In her mind she was right and I had to respect that.

I felt surprisingly relaxed considering the day was as stressful as any day could be. I'd almost forgotten I'd been away from Mum's funeral for less than an hour such was the intensity of what Jessie and I had been talking about. I was still slumped on the settee and whilst Jessie was out of the room and my focus of attention wasn't on her my eyes were drawn to the photographs that littered the walls and mantelpiece. There were a few more than there had been and I guessed that Dad had got out as many of Mum as he possibly could. I hadn't spent any time with him the previous evening choosing to keep my distance but I wished I had because most of the photographs included me. A lump ushered itself to my throat and I forcibly held back my tears. I was sure there were pictures of just Mum's image but the fact that Dad had chosen to include me in his makeshift shrine to Mum made me realise that it was time for us to make our peace.

"Jessie!" I called out sadly, "come here."
She did as I asked, stopping in the doorway. She didn't look as angry as she had when she left but there was still something in her expression that said she was desperately unhappy.

"Come here," I said again, "I want you."
I wasn't quite sure what I meant by what I said and I was even less sure how Jessie was going to take it. She approached me anyway without saying a word and sat down. I pulled her close squeezing a little bit too hard and quite forcefully kissed her full on the lips. I must have been too rough as she backed away and wiped her mouth with the back of her hand. She shook her head as she looked at me.

"You stupid bastard," she said, but I knew that she didn't mean it nastily. We fell back into the softness of the settee and renewed our passion for each other. It felt so right, better than anything I had ever experienced. I never thought anything would be better than Alice and maybe time had put paid to those feelings. I would always love Alice, there would never be any doubt about that but my fears that Jessie was just going to be a replacement weren't materialising. Jessie was her own person, a stronger personality than her mother and I was falling in love with her for herself rather than an image in my mind.

CHAPTER ELEVEN

We didn't see Dad before we both went to bed. It wasn't late but I found myself drifting off to sleep and thought it best that I settled down for the night. The day had been traumatic to say the least and in the back of my mind was the fear that talking to Dad wouldn't be productive and the best time to talk would be in the morning.

The evening with Jessie had been fun and she had managed to bring a smile back to my face. In little over twenty-four hours she had managed to change not my opinion of her but the way I saw our future. Maybe I was coming to terms with what I had done to Tom and begun to realise what a mistake that had been. I was so confused at the time I thought I was making the world a better place for not only me but Mary and Mulvey as well.

The thoughts of Tom brought a fresh problem to my mind. How was he going to react when he got out of hospital and more importantly how was he going to react if he ever found out I was seeing Jessie.

I tried to put it out of my mind; it was something

to deal with at another time if and when it actually happened. The moment was about Jessie and me and the warmth of her body was the only thing I was interested in. It was something I had to make the most of; I wouldn't be getting anything like it in jail.

We made love again in the cramped single bed and fell asleep almost immediately afterwards. I slept lightly, thoughts of Dean were lodged at the back of my mind and with Jessie there as well I was conscious that I had somebody to protect.

At about eleven thirty I heard what I thought was a disturbance outside. I leapt out of bed and rushed to the window peering out into the darkness. Someone was trying to get in the house. First instincts told me it was Dean but as my eyes quickly adjusted to the gloom of the night I realised it was Dad. He seemed to be struggling so I pulled on a pair of trousers and went downstairs to let him in.

He almost fell over the step as I opened the door. There was something unfamiliar about his manner.

I couldn't believe it...he was drunk.

I never thought I would see the day and I couldn't help but smile at his predicament.

"Don't just stand there, help me." Dad slurred as he took a step towards me stumbling as he went.

I reached out to stop his imminent fall and he clung on to me laughing. I didn't know what to say so I just babbled.

"You look like you had a good time!"

Dad laughed again and said a few incoherent things. I hadn't a clue what he was talking about and just agreed with him.

"I think we'd better get you into bed." I said as Jessie appeared by my side.

"Is he o.k?" Jessie asked of me rather than pose the question to Dad. She wouldn't have got any sense out of him anyway. I shrugged my shoulders.

"I think he needs to sleep it off, give me a hand to get him upstairs."

We struggled for about ten minutes before we managed to get him to his room where he immediately crashed out on his bed. I removed his shoes and jacket and placed a blanket over him before leaving him alone.

Jessie and I returned to bed chatting for a while mainly about Dad and what sort of night he had appeared to have. Jessie seemed to think that he had been pleased to see me and that it could be the kick-start to getting our lives back to normal. I said that I'd rather wait and see. I wasn't sure whether it was just him being so unaccustomed to alcohol; everything might be so different in the morning.

The morning I was expecting never happened because suddenly, as I was talking, something came crashing through the bedroom window hitting Jessie full in the face. She collapsed to the floor screaming and I could see blood seeping through her fingers as she clutched at her face. I saw the brick lying next to her and I looked back through the shattered window to try and see who had thrown it.

I didn't really need to. It was bound to be Dean.

He was stood halfway down the path staring up at the damage he had caused, a smug look of delight on his face. Instinctively I dashed downstairs to confront him.

"You bastard!" I yelled lunging towards him but he was quicker than I imagined him to be and sidestepped swinging a fist towards my head. It connected and it was hard. I lost my balance and fell headlong into the bushes that lined the path. Dean was on to me in a flash punching me repeatedly in the head and body. I put out my hands in self-defence but it was no use, I had no chance. I was badly dazed as Dean stood up this time aiming kicks at my increasingly battered body. He stamped down hard on my legs and arms many times, once so forcibly I swear I heard one of my bones crack. I was shouting and so was he. Lights switched on in the house next door and momentarily distracted Dean, he looked around before taking an almighty swing with his foot sending it smashing into my face.

Then it stopped. Dean had taken off.

I tried to open my eyes; everything was blurred. I started to swallow blood and urged at the sickly taste. I felt hands pulling at my shoulders and for a moment feared that Dean was back. I tried to move away but I was in too much pain and resigned myself to a further beating. It didn't happen; instead I heard Dad's voice. I tried to answer but the words didn't come out, I could barely move my lips. Dad tried lifting me up but as he did so I let out an agonised moan.

"The ambulance is on its way." I heard him say.

I tried asking him how Jessie was but he couldn't understand my mumbles. I could think quite clearly and I was really angry with myself, my priority should have been Jessie but I'd brushed past her in my desire to get at Dean. What must she think of me? I didn't know if I could face her.

I heard the ambulance screech to a halt, its siren cutting out as it stopped. I was aware of shadows and voices as eventually I was lifted onto a stretcher and carried towards the waiting vehicle. The interior light of the ambulance hurt my eyes and it took a while to adjust to the sudden brightness. When I did I recognised the slight figure of someone sat opposite to where I was lying. It was Jessie. I knew it was her even though her head was swathed in bandages, bandages that were stained bright red. Dad was sat next to her, a comforting arm around her shoulder, and I wondered how he had managed to sober up so quickly. I was glad he had otherwise I would have still been lying semi conscious on the ground.

I was being treated as we raced towards hospital and in less than fifteen minutes I was wheeled on a trolley through the emergency departments doors. I didn't see Jessie again as we were put into separate cubicles for the nursing staff to treat our injuries and after what seemed like hours I was taken upstairs to a ward for the remainder of the night.

CHAPTER TWELVE

Dad visited briefly to check that I was o.k. and told me a few things that I didn't know. The x-rays I'd had taken showed that I hadn't broken any bones but I would probably have to stay in hospital for about a week. Jessie had been kept in too but on another ward.

Her injuries were bad...a broken nose and deep cuts under her right eye. I wanted to see her to apologise for leaving her lying in my bedroom but I couldn't move from my bed. Dad told me he would go and see her again before he went home to let her know that I wanted to talk to her. He suggested that maybe she could walk up and see me in the morning. I mumbled my thanks.

I had an uncomfortable night, the nurses on duty tended to my cries of pain whenever it was necessary but for the most part they left me alone. I was still in agony the next morning but could sense feeling was returning to my limbs. I was thankful that nothing had been broken especially my legs; I don't know how I would have coped with that, at least whatever damage Dean had inflicted was not long term.

Bastard!

He would have been laughing his head off wherever he was but I bet he hadn't realised what he had done to Jessie. He wouldn't have known she was there and even less likely to know that the brick he'd thrown had hit her directly in the face. The only thing the incident had shown me was just how dangerous Dean had become. Even Tom, no matter what I thought of him as a person, had never been as psychotic as to beat the living daylights out of anyone. Sure we'd had a fight in the past and I had come out of it on top but it was nothing compared to the violence Dean had shown. I wasn't going soft on my feelings of hate towards Tom after all he was still a murderer and a rapist and had to pay for his crimes. I wanted to make sure that he did but I needed the support of both Jessie and Mary before I could do anything about that and that support was something I didn't think I would ever get especially from Mary.

I was getting angry again.

Maybe Jessie was right; maybe it would have been better if I had killed Tom. Dean wouldn't have hurt either of us then and I would be safely locked up in prison. Even Dad may not have been targeted by Dean in his efforts to get at me. Maybe the time had come to try again and this time succeed. Maybe killing Tom would put an end to the extra suffering I had created. It was a ridiculous thought but it played on my mind and I was slowly convincing myself it was the only option. I no longer cared what happened to me. Maybe it wasn't Tom who was the catalyst for all the misery maybe it was me. If I was out of the way then everybody else could start getting their own lives back to normality.

Jessie didn't come to see me that day and that pushed me even closer to the edge, I was almost at breaking point and the insane thoughts that were careering out of control around my head weren't helping. All I could focus on was ending Tom's life and planning how to do it. I had to take action as soon as possible. Maybe being where I was, lying in the same hospital as Tom was an omen, a blessing in disguise. Maybe I was in hospital for the sole reason of killing Tom. One thing was sure I was scared of going into the outside world again. I was scared of Dean.

Jessie's arrival on my ward the next day gave me the idea for how I was to get at Tom. Being a patient herself she had wandered up to my bed unchallenged and the way my mind was working it instantly occurred to me that I could do the same. I doubted that Tom would have any sort of police guard, after all I had been under curfew and now badly beaten up...what sort of threat did I pose to anybody.

I didn't mention anything to Jessie that may have given her cause for concern. I thought about asking if her Dad was still in intensive care but decided against it, I was sure that if he wasn't she would have already told me.

With her help I tried walking up and down the ward and although it was extremely painful to do I knew that another twenty-four hours rest would reduce my pain even further. I made up my mind to pay Tom a visit the following day.

I spent a couple of hours with Jessie aware that it was possibly the last time I would se her for a while. She was being allowed home later that day and although I was fearful about her going out without me I made her promise that if Dean caused any problems with her to go and stay with Dad. We kissed goodbye and parted with a smile. Even though I knew what I was going to do I hoped that one day I would see her smile again.

I slept well that night. In my own fucked up world I was content that everything was going to end up with everybody being happy and all my problems would be solved.

I got out of bed as soon as I woke grabbing the crutches I'd acquired and hobbled off towards the toilet. I needed a couple of hours walking practice before I went to find Tom.

I'd decided to get it over with as early as possible, for one thing the wards seemed quieter in the morning and with afternoon and evening visiting hours it made sense that with less people around my task would be easier.

I wandered into the corridor outside the ward and checked the board by the lifts to find out where intensive care was. I was relieved that it was on the floor directly below mine, at least I wouldn't have to walk too far.

By nine thirty breakfast had been served and cleared away. It was this time of the day that was the most boring but for me it was going to be the most eventful. The doctors didn't usually begin their rounds until eleven and I saw it as the chance to make my move. Hobbling off towards the lift I spoke briefly to the nurse who was sat behind the ward reception desk. Little did she know that the smile on my face belied the truth and it wasn't because I told her I was happy to be mobile once more.

I pressed the button to direct the lift to the floor I wanted and five seconds later I was there. I looked around for the sign that pointed me towards the intensive care unit and I slowly made my way down the corridor. I didn't pass a single sole and was amazed that nobody seemed to be on duty.

Maybe there was and they were just attending to a patient. Hopefully, if that was the case, it wasn't Tom.

There were six separate units and I carefully peered through the glass on the door of the first one immediately ducking out of sight as I almost came face to face with the missing nurses. By now my heartbeat was increasing rapidly in anticipation and I quickly looked into the next unit.

It was Tom's.

I felt a little worried that it was the one next door to where the nursing staff were working but then remembered Tom was still in a coma, he wasn't likely to cry out.

Quietly I closed the door behind me and looked at Tom for a moment. He looked peaceful just lying there connected by tubes and wires to a number of life maintaining machines. I thought my best bet was just to unplug them but realised an alarm system would trigger the nurses into action.

Damn.

The realisation made me aware that anything I did would set off some sort of alarm. He was plugged into life saving equipment. I had to be quick if I wanted him dead. I looked around the room for something, anything that could cause instant death. A fire extinguisher was fixed to the wall next to the door. I picked it up and it felt heavy enough to crush his skull with. I had to put both crutches down to carry it towards Tom's bed.

"Say goodnight you bastard!" I yelled as I lifted the canister above my head.

It was heavier than I thought and my tired legs couldn't take the strain. I fell backwards crashing into a trolley holding all kinds of medical equipment sending it flying across the room. The door burst open almost immediately and I caught a glimpse of the nurse just before the extinguisher made contact with my head.

CHAPTER THIRTEEN

Until my court case Jessie was the only person I knew that I ever saw after that and it was through her that I found out that Dad had completely washed his hands of me. She had stayed in contact with him because she told me she had to. Where there was contact there was always hope, the hope that one day there would be understanding and then, hopefully, forgiveness.

After knocking myself out I was put in a high security single ward, two policemen permanently on guard as much for my own security as for any threat that I posed to Tom. My wounds healed quickly and it was three days later that I was moved out and placed in a remand centre where I was to stay until the date of my trial was known. I hadn't done myself any favours and the newspapers had a field day for a while dishing any dirt they could find out about me. Old girlfriends came out of the shadows of the past to make up any stories they could just to make a fast buck for themselves. I wasn't in a position to deny their allegations eventually ignoring all the bullshit I was hearing not only from Jessie but also from the comings and goings of other prisoners being held on remand.

Jessie was a godsend to me at that time. I was able to talk to her freely on the days she was allowed to visit and I convinced her quite easily that I wasn't the person the gutter press were making me out to be. The one thing that I was thankful for was that they hadn't got their claws into her and my previous relationship with Alice. I half expected Dean to mouth off to the tabloids about it but I guessed his sexual preferences were a bit of a stumbling block for him as well as Alice being his mother.

Jessie kept me in contact with the outside world as best she could and I was lucky enough to be able to make a couple of phone calls a week to her in addition to seeing her on a fortnightly basis.

She told me that Mulvey had been in contact with her and wanted to visit me to explain a few things. Apparently he wanted to apologise for turning me in the first time I was arrested and if there was anything he could do to help. He offered me the services of his solicitor but I told Jessie to ask him to leave me alone and that I didn't need his help.

I upset Jessie on that visit as I told her that I would be pleading guilty and had to take whatever punishment was given to me. She begged and begged me to reconsider and choose another route, to at least plead not guilty. I said I couldn't, that I had done what I had done deliberately and didn't want to discuss it any further. She knew I had my reasons but still couldn't understand why I wouldn't tell anyone.

"I want you out of there!" She cried as she left. The date of my trial came through and you couldn't have made up a worse day for me to have it on. It was due to start on my birthday. The anniversary of the very fucking reason I was going to be doing time. I was going to be in a good mood that day.

I wallowed in my own self pity for the next few days hardly speaking to anybody, I didn't even bother phoning Jessie even though I had credit on my phone card and she was a little apprehensive talking to me the following week when she came to visit. It was her last visit before the trial and I told her that it was the end, that I didn't want her to wait. I didn't want her to visit after I had been sentenced. I hated myself for saying all the things I was saying but I couldn't see that there was any point. She had the right to a proper life even if I didn't.

"Don't ever tell me what to do," she shouted at me as she left, "I have my own mind just as you have yours...I'll be outside the day you're released!"

The trial lasted two days. I did enlist the services of a solicitor but that was just for the legal process. I was pleading guilty and couldn't care less what anyone said on my behalf. I took the stand the final time to listen to the judge summing up and barely heard the sentence. Seven years. To me it was just time.

I glanced up at the public gallery for the first time since I'd been in court. Everybody was there. Jessie, Mary, Mulvey and even Dad. Tom was out fully recovered and shouting abuse at the top of his voice. I heard his threats that he would be waiting and then it would be my turn. I was numb with the whole experience but managed eye contact with Jessie. She was crying but still mouthed the words...I love you...at me. I gave her a half-hearted smile. I wanted to shout out to her that I loved her too but just picked up my bag of personal possessions as the usher led me from the courtroom.

I didn't know what to expect from that moment on. I was led to a holding cell beneath the courtrooms and the vile stench of sick and urine greeted me as the door was opened. It struck me that the cell hadn't been cleaned for a long time if ever.

My case had been the first to finish that day and I had to stay in the stinking cell until everyone else had been dealt with before any of us could be transferred to prison.

At various times during the next few hours I was joined by a selection of convicted criminals and my first impressions were that they were all of an untrustworthy nature, but where did that leave me? I'd been convicted of attempted murder so maybe that made me worse than them. I greeted the first two with a simple hello but didn't pursue a conversation. I just wanted to be out of there and settled into what was going to be my new home.

Eventually we were led out to board our transport to prison, a huge white bus the insides of which made it look like a mobile prison. What else did I expect? I was a prisoner and had to accept that I was going to be treated like one. The one good thing about the bus was that it didn't smell as much as the cell I'd just left.

An hour later we had reached our destination and we were led from the bus to the reception area where each of us was processed in turn. The undignified embarrassment of the strip search, the photo shoot where everyone did their best to look as threatening as possible and finally the issue of prison clothes. The shirt and trousers were bearable but the thought of the underwear already worn by countless other prisoners was hard to take. It was the stomach churning moment that made my punishment become real and it took all of my willpower to suppress myself from throwing up everything my body contained.

CHAPTER FOURTEEN

That first night my opinion of prison changed for good and I realised my sentence would be mentally much longer than seven years, to me it would seem like life. The sound of the cell door slamming shut and the bolts sliding into place shook me almost rigid. The harshness and coldness of it all was a far cry from my time served on remand. Any bad times I had thought I'd had in the past hadn't in any way prepared me for what lay ahead.

After being issued with our second hand clothing we were informed there would be an induction for us to attend the following morning where everything about prison life and what was expected of us would be explained. We were then led into the prison itself. I didn't know how the other new arrivals felt or whether they had been inside or not before but I found the experience intimidating and for want of a better word disgusting. It was quite the filthiest place I'd ever seen in my life. Cleanliness certainly wasn't an important part of the daily life in this part of the world. We followed the guard up two flights of iron stairs and I was told to wait with another inmate outside one of the cells. Once the door was opened the guard told us to enter. My cellmate immediately put his belongings on the bottom mattress of the bunk bed set against the wall. Not your first time inside then I thought to myself as he immediately made himself at home. I looked around the cell; it was just as dirty as the rest as the prison.

I wanted out, I wanted to go home. I turned back towards the door just as it slammed shut. The reality started to bite deep.

"First timer?"

My cellmate spoke, the first words I'd heard him utter since leaving Crown Court.

"I can always tell, bag of nerves and shit scared!"

I tried to answer his first question but it didn't seem like he was interested in what I had to say, he just carried on talking.

"My sixth stretch, doing twelve this time, armed robbery. Dunno why I took the gun, could never use it, could never kill anyone. What you in for?"

"Attempted murder!"

Silence greeted my answer as my fellow captive just stared at me. I tried to imagine what he was thinking but guessed that I wasn't any different to anyone he had seen before judging by the amount of times he had been inside. If I was going to be sharing a cell with him then I at least had to try and make friends. I offered my hand towards him but he didn't return the gesture. He grunted that his name was Badger on account that he hunted at night. I smiled inwardly; at least he had a sense of humour.

The conversation didn't have any chance to progress any further as our cell door was opened once more and an officer yelled that tea was ready. I followed Badger's lead and grabbed the plate and cup that had been left on my mattress and joined the queue of prisoners as they made their way to the dining hall.

The food was dire, a ladleful of some sort of meat and vegetables that was just slopped onto the plate. I didn't dare ask what it was meant to be just mumbled my thanks and turned to face the rapidly filling dining hall.

I felt the eyes of everybody burning into me as I made my way to an empty table and sat down. My meal tasted as revolting as it looked but I forced myself to eat it. The food at the remand centre was five star gourmet compared to the crap that was now in my stomach. I wondered how I was going to keep it down. Barely two hours into my sentence I realised that prison was no holiday camp and I was sure that there was worse to come.

It was six o'clock, tea was over and we all had to return to our cells for the night. Our plates and cutlery were our own responsibility and with nowhere to wash them they had to stay dirty until the next morning. No wonder the place was so filthy with such scant regard to hygiene. As we were locked in our cells from six in the evening we were each issued with a bucket that acted as our toilet. It was the most humiliating experience of my life the first time I used it crouching down to empty my bowels. It wouldn't have been so bad had I been on my own but with Badger watching I felt as though I'd ended up in hell. He later informed me that most inmates wrapped their excrement in paper and chucked them out of the window and if I didn't want the cell to stink then I should do the same. The thought of that was too much for me and I couldn't bring myself to do what he suggested.

Lights out was at nine thirty. I'd had some sleepless nights in the past but that first night was quite possibly the worst. As soon as the lights went out the noise started. Shouting and screaming and crying. I was no longer in prison I was in a lunatic asylum. How long would it be before I was the same as everyone else? How long before I too was at breaking point? I gave myself a week.

If the lack of sleep that first night was bad it was nothing compared to the horror of the following morning. The ritual of slopping out, washing our plates and cutlery, using the toilet and showering all taking place in the same area. If there was anywhere in the world that should have been rife with disease then that was it and I had seven years of it to look forward to. It wasn't any wonder that most prisoners chose to chuck their shit out of the window at night.

The floor was awash with water and waste, not all of it was the remains of last night's food. I joined in the free for all, there seemed to be no queuing system in operation just a case of who got to the tap first. I was determined not to face this horror too often. Washing my plates had to be done every day but slopping out was something I could do without. I began to imagine what life had been like in the Middle Ages and was half expecting a rat to jump out at me at any moment.

Breakfast came and went, the food was slightly more edible and then it was back to our cells. I had always been led to believe that being in prison wasn't much different to being outside with the opportunity to mix with fellow inmates all day long but it was a million miles from the truth, the only interaction I was to get would be at meal times and the nightmare that was slopping out and I didn't think that was a place to want to stop for a chat.

We did have, I was to learn later, a recreation time where we could exercise or rather walk around the yard and it was there on my first visit that I noticed just how many shit parcels were thrown out night after night. I was careful not to tread in any otherwise I would just be transferring it back to my cell.

I kept myself to myself for the first couple of days out of choice. I wasn't normally an ignorant person I just needed time on my own to think. I was determined not to receive any visitors or even phone home to see how things were. I remembered that Dad had, according to Jessie, washed his hands of me but he was in court to hear the judge pass sentence and I couldn't work out what that meant. Had he really given up on me? Or was he trying to show me that I still had his support? I didn't care any more. I just wanted to be forgotten.

CHAPTER FIFTEEN

I had been inside for five days and nothing had changed. The revolting food, the filth that was slopping out and the noise ridden sleepless nights. I was shattered, depressed and angry.

Badger had seemed a bit wary of me those first few days and I could only guess it was because the first thing I had said to him was that I was inside for attempted murder, although I was pretty sure he had met some criminals in the past that were a lot more dangerous than me. He didn't know the circumstances of my crime and I felt that he was judging me harshly. If he was scared of me then he was very wrong and I needed to clear the air with him. Five days of virtual silence between us was long enough so I took a chance and asked him in respect of his experience how I could deal with prison life.

He offered me a cigarette from the packet clutched in his hand and although I refused it was the first moment in my life that I had actually felt like smoking one.

He recounted tales of his own experiences in jail, not all of them in any way pleasant to listen to, and I got the impression that my first five days were nothing compared to what I still might have to go through. Eventually Badger finished his trip down memory lane and told me the only way I could deal with it was to accept it. I didn't know if I could.

The following day was mail day. The one day a week that us prisoners, apart from visiting day, had any contact with the outside world. I had one letter and I knew at once who had sent it. I took it back to my cell where I sat on my bunk staring at it. I didn't want to open it; I didn't want to hear what Jessie had to say. It was quite a thick envelope and I estimated that she had written at least a dozen pages. Even though I had said I no longer wanted any contact with her I knew she was someone who wasn't going to take any notice. It must have been an hour later when I finally opened it and began to read.

The first bit was difficult, all her feelings poured out in a mish-mash of emotion. It was a bit incoherent but I could sense the deepness of her feelings and what she was trying to say. I had to be strong...I didn't want it to affect me; I was determined not to go back on my word. If I could get through the first few letters she sent without replying to any of them then I felt she would finally get the message that I didn't want to see or hear from her any more. The few lines begging to let her visit, begging for a phone call were the hardest to read and I felt sorry that I was putting her through so much heartache. I was a bastard and I knew it.

I stopped reading for a while promising myself I would pick it up again later in the day, I couldn't deal straightaway with all that she was saying and my mood wasn't helped with the return of Badger beaming and clutching a wad of mail from his wife and children.

"It's the best thing about being inside," he said, "knowing that there's someone on the outside waiting."

I felt like telling him to fuck off. If he had a loving family on the outside then what the fuck was he doing? To return to prison as many times as he had done was nothing short of stupidity. My attitude was that I had let people down and didn't deserve their love or support. Dad was the only person who was doing the right thing by washing his hands of me. Even though he had shown up in court I didn't think that I would ever hear from him again.

It was lunchtime and I left Badger and his good mood alone in our cell. I wandered into the dining hall to see what disgusting concoction was to be dished up in the name of cuisine. Unsurprisingly it looked awful. A pale and unappetising shepherd's pie and a piece of sponge covered with the lumpiest custard I had ever seen. I took my tray to an empty table and devoured the food, not with any relish but with the desire to get it past the taste buds of my mouth as quickly as possible. I washed away any lingering after taste with a drink of water.

I looked around the hall.

As with every other mealtime there were a few fellow inmates who seemed to be glaring at me. I didn't know what they thought they were staring at. I had only really spoken to Badger since I'd been inside as I didn't want to strike up any friendships with people I didn't trust. I hadn't any idea who they were and what they were in for but their outward appearance frightened the life out of me. If I could serve my sentence by keeping myself to myself then chances were that I wouldn't get into any trouble. After hearing some of the stories that Badger had told me I thought I would be better off that way. Little did I know then that I was only alienating myself and it wasn't long before I found out how much.

Lunchtime that day was followed by an hours exercise in the yard. It was an experience that I had found the most pleasurable since I'd been there. The feelings of fresh air on my face gave me a sense of freedom and the belief that all was well in the world. I wandered around the yard oblivious to anything that was going on around me. Groups of up to half a dozen men were stood at various points and it was when I passed one of these groups that I vaguely heard someone calling out. I wasn't aware that they were trying to get my attention until two of the group moved to stand in front of me. One of them who was more than twice the size of me spoke.

"Dave wants a word," was all he said and I was led back to where Dave was.

The man looked positively ferocious, like a twenty stone pit-bull, and if the looks of some of the other inmates frightened me then Dave absolutely terrified me. It was as Dave spoke that I realised my desire to be inconspicuous hadn't been a good idea. I had unintentionally ruffled a few feathers by my reluctance to mix. It was a friendly warning...for now.

Back in my cell I demanded a cigarette from Badger and although I choked on my first few drags by the time I had finished I felt that the fear caused by Dave and his cronies had subsided somewhat.

Even though we were prisoners we had a weekly allowance of a couple of pounds that we were able to spend on anything available in the shop. It was meant for a few luxuries to make our hell a little more bearable. I hadn't bought anything up until then but on finishing the cigarette I immediately went and bought myself a packet. I returned one to Badger who then informed me that everything in prison was only borrowed but accrued interest. He meant that I had to give him two. I knew I still had a lot to learn about prison life.

CHAPTER SIXTEEN

I took my threats from Dave on board immediately and I made sure that every time I spotted him or any of his group I would acknowledge them.

My first packet of cigarettes didn't last long. In an effort to appease them I offered them all a smoke and I didn't expect any in return. They all readily accepted except one who strangely just asked for the foil out of the box. I found his request a little odd but let him have his wish.

The days after the incident in the yard seemed to change me. Everything about prison was still the same filth ridden hell but my turning to smoking had somehow seemed to chill me out. Maybe I had done what Badger had told me to do and accepted my fate.

I had finished reading Jessie's letter and I was fully aware of how much hatred was waiting for me when I finally emerged from prison. Tom and Dean were vowing vengeance and Dad had had one more visit from Dean. My hope that he would stop hadn't materialised and I prayed to myself that Dad's suffering would soon come to an end.

"Bastard!" I yelled loud enough for Badger to sit up and take notice.

I spilled the beans to him about what was happening to Dad and he did his best to reassure me that everything would be o.k. If Dean carried on victimising Dad then he too would eventually end up inside.

At three o'clock our cell was opened and we were each informed that we had a visitor. Badger was elated and rushed off to meet his. I refused to leave my cell. I knew it was going to be Jessie waiting but I was still adamant with myself that I had to be cruel to be kind. She had to start to accept that I wasn't there any more.

An hour later Badger was back, smiling. His wife had been to see him and had brought their youngest daughter with her. It was enough to get him through the next couple of weeks he told me.

"If you set yourself things to look forward to then time passes by quickly."

It was good advice but I replied that I wouldn't ever have anything to look forward to.

"What about the girl who was waiting?" he asked.

He had worked out that Jessie was my visitor as she was the only one waiting at an empty table.

I shrugged my shoulders.

"She knows I don't want to see her."

I lit a cigarette, drawing on it for about five seconds taking the cloud of burning tobacco fumes deep into my lungs where I held it for an age before releasing the smoke into the cramped cell. I thought of Jessie and what she must have been thinking as she made her way back home. I wondered if Dean had told Tom about our relationship and hoped he would show he had a decent side to his character by having not done so. I couldn't bear the thought of her having to face any more of Tom's anger than she had to.

I wondered too about how Tom had reacted to the knowledge that Dean was gay. Had he even remembered the last scene he saw before I had plunged the knife into his chest? Jessie's letter had told me that they both wanted revenge but were they together on that quest or both on separate missions. I hoped that with me being out of the way for so long then Tom and Dean would have their own issue to sort out first and God knows what the outcome of that was likely to be.

I was in a reflective mood as I continued to draw on my cigarette, putting myself in the position of everybody I knew and how they were handling the aftermath of what I had done. Mulvey, for all his good intentions, I decided I couldn't care less about. I had wanted help from him but all he had done was turn me in.

I flicked the ash that was building up into the ashtray and took one last drag before stubbing out the cigarette. I wanted another but with one packet having to last all week I had to ration myself. I could understand why most of the other smokers rolled their own and thought that it was time I did the same.

I pictured Mary next. God, what must she be going through? I had even stupidly told Tom that Mikey was his son. In the cold light of day I realised that I might be responsible for causing even greater grief in her life. What if Tom paid her a visit? What if...Jesus...what if he raped her again?

I had to stop thinking. I needed something to occupy my mind to rid myself of the guilt that was beginning to build up. Thankfully it was teatime and I disappeared towards the dining hall knowing full well that whatever was served up would definitely give me something else to think about.

One thing that happened with regularity, especially on our wing, was the comings and goings of prisoners. The lifers, as expected, were there to stay but others coming to the end of their sentence were either moved to a less secure jail or to a lower category wing in the same prison. I hadn't taken much notice of it as it was just another part of prison life. However that day it was different, that day it brought the past back to haunt me.

"Reynolds!"

The voice came from behind me in the queue. I turned and had one of the biggest shocks of my life. Although he had aged somewhat I still recognised him. Someone I had grown up with, someone who had hung around with Tom and Alice and me. Someone who was there on my sixteenth birthday. Someone who knew everything.

Tony Watson hadn't been the most vociferous person in our group but he was the one who was most easily manipulated by Tom and carried out his demands without a second thought. It was almost as if he was Tom's second in command, not that he needed one. I knew I was in trouble.

I left the queue without waiting for any food and returned to my cell. I was sweating heavily such was my panic and I quickly lit a cigarette in an effort to calm my nerves.

Shit. What was he doing here? It seemed to my paranoid mind that he had been sent by Tom. The way he spoke and smiled had struck more fear into me than Dave had the first week I was inside. I began to feel grateful that I had made a friend of Dave and decided to ask if there was any way that

I could be protected. It was a coward's way out but something I needed to do.

Suddenly I heard a whistle, the signal from the prison officers that a fight had broken out. The whistle had two meanings one to attract the attention of other officers to the scene of the fight and the other to instruct all prisoners back to their cells.

Badger came rushing in almost immediately.

"It's Dave," he informed me and instantly my hopes of protection were dashed.

There had been a bit of friction between two groups of inmates and a debt hadn't been paid. Dave had decided action was needed in sorting it out. It took six guards to bring him down but not before he had dished out quite a beating to the debtor. Dave was a lifer and it didn't matter to him that he was hauled off to solitary. A debt was a debt and not something to be tolerated. My mind flashed back to my first meeting with Dave and I was thankful that I had escaped with a warning. Trouble was it didn't help my impending problem and I discussed it with Badger. He didn't know what to suggest. Prison wasn't the best place to hide from someone so I had to be thankful that I was locked in my cell for such a long time every day.

I stuck by Badger's side for the next week, keeping

my eye on Watson. His eyes were also on me and he maintained a stupid grin on his face. He seemed to be mixing well with a lot of people and I knew something was brewing. I began thinking that maybe I should just let him get on with it, to take my beating and then he would be happy that he had done his duty for Tom.

It happened the next morning and it wasn't a beating it was worse, so much worse that that.

I was out of bed later than normal and when I reached the slopping out area most of the other inmates had already finished. The mess was incredibly bad and the stench something else. The fact that we had had fish the previous evening may have had something to do with that. I walked across the floor, which was by then ankle deep in water, to reach the tap to flush out my bucket. I raised my eyes in acknowledgment to the last couple using the tap before they left to leave me on my own. After a minute I heard footsteps in the water behind me but didn't think anything of it as I just presumed that it was someone else even later to slopping out than I was.

I heard voices as at least another two prisoners joined us and I heard the toilet door open and close. Then everything went quiet, too quiet. I had finished cleaning my bucket and turned round to make the trek back to my cell.

Watson was two yards behind me and two of his friends were stood as if guarding the door. I dropped my bucket in fear as Watson grabbed my arm. I winced, closing my eyes tightly waiting for the punches to land but they never came instead Watson led me across the room towards the toilet door kicking me hard on the back of my legs as we reached it. I shouted out in pain and fell to my knees on the floor. The toilet door opened and I was confronted by someone naked from the waist down, his erect penis barely two inches from my face. Watson grabbed my hair and pulled backwards, the force of which made my mouth open wide and in a split second my worst nightmare began to materialise as the erect organ was forced deep inside. I tried to pull away but Watson held me firmly in place as the man in front of me thrust himself in and out of my mouth. I gagged as he kept hitting the back of my throat until finally his fluid flooded into me. He held himself fully inside until he'd finished then pulled himself out. I tried to spit out everything but he put one hand over my mouth and with the other gripped my nose. Watson tipped my head backwards. I couldn't breathe; the way they were holding me gave me no choice...I had to swallow.

They had achieved their aim and let go before hastily running out into the prison corridor leaving me alone. I desperately reached into my mouth trying to scrape out anything I could. I rammed my fingers down my throat in a vain attempt to make myself vomit. Nothing happened. I rushed to the slopping out tap not caring what I was stepping in and stuck my head under it. The water gushed out drenching me but it didn't matter I had to flush out my body to get rid of the vileness I'd just swallowed. It took about a minute until finally, thankfully, I threw up.

CHAPTER SEVENTEEN

I was lying naked, shivering, under the covers of my bed. The revulsion of what I'd been put through was making me angry. I'd staggered back to my cell drenched attracting the laughter of many of my fellow inmates. They probably thought I'd just fallen over and to them it must have looked comical. I wasn't laughing. Why hadn't they just beaten me up, broken my arms, legs, anything but that. It must have been Tom that set it up. I imagined that Watson had deliberately got himself into trouble to get into the same prison; maybe he'd already been inside somewhere else and got himself a transfer. I didn't know I hadn't seen him for years but as he was a friend of Tom I knew that anything was possible.

I managed to smoke all my remaining cigarettes in the first hour after being forced through the degrading assault. Badger had arrived back at the cell just as I'd clambered into my bunk. He took one look at my pile of sodden clothes and one look at me and knew at once that something serious had happened. He tried asking me but I wasn't answering his questions. He called in prison officers to see me but I refused to talk to them as well. If I wasn't going to speak then they weren't going to help. They left the cell and told me to get over it. One thing I'd learnt from Badger and Dave was that prisoners sorted out their own problems, talking to screws wasn't looked upon lightly by other cons. Any friendliness was taboo and dealt with violently. I didn't want that after what I'd been through. Badger knew who was responsible for what had happened because I'd told him my fears when I first spotted Watson and I heard him telling me that it would be sorted. I didn't try to stop him.

Three days later I came out of my cell, somehow Watson had gone and I never found out what had happened to him.

I wasn't the same person ever again. That incident changed me as a person forever. I came out of my cell with an attitude. I was no longer going to be scared of anyone; no one would ever again give me any shit. I was angry and nobody was going to get in my way. I remembered Badger telling me that if I had something to look forward to then time would go quickly. Well now I did have something to look forward to...getting out and getting Tom.

I'd received yet another letter from Jessie. This

time it was short just begging me to see her when she came to visit. She said she had something to tell me that could only be said face to face. It didn't matter to me what it was I still wasn't going to talk to her.

Strangely later that day I was called into the office to see the governor. I assumed that it was something to do with the incident regarding Watson but it wasn't. The governor had some heartbreaking news for me. Dad was dead, he had hung himself.

To say I was devastated was an understatement, I was completely overwhelmed. My new found anger desperately needed an outlet and I needed to let off steam somewhere. To my shame I went to the dining room and trashed it. Tables and chairs went flying everywhere until I was restrained and put into a cell on my own. The doctor was called in to see me and gave me some sort of sedative to calm me down. It may have worked on my body but it certainly didn't work on my fucked up mind.

My anger had increased tenfold but was now directed more towards Dean than Tom. Dean was responsible totally for my father's death. Suicide is the final answer to emotional pain and Dean had obviously driven Dad to the point of no return.

Sympathy had never been a strong emotional trait for a prison officer, to them we were just scum. No matter what offence we were inside for we were all tarred with the same brush. Murdering, thieving pieces of shit and we were all treated as such. However family death is different. It's a fact of life that we all experience it at some point and even prison officers sometimes show they have a human side to their otherwise arrogant, ignorant nature. I was treated with remarkable humanity in the days I was kept in solitary, continually informed about funeral arrangements and generally pampered to the point of friendliness. Even the food was more palatable than what was normally served.

I was kept in solitary until the day of the funeral, I had been given permission to go because it was close family but I was still dreading it. The drugs the doctor had been giving me had rendered me pretty lifeless but I still had to go through the whole service handcuffed to an officer.

There was a police presence on duty at the church just as there had been at Mum's funeral but by now the media were no longer interested in me. I'd been convicted ages ago and was no longer deemed good copy.

I was at the church early before many people had arrived and when I spotted Jessie I had a shock, she was very obviously pregnant. I knew at once that that was what she meant when she said she had something to tell me. I wasn't allowed to speak to her but I got the message when she pointed at her stomach and then pointed at me. There was something else for me to get my head around. I was going to be a father.

CHAPTER EIGHTEEN

The shock of seeing a pregnant Jessie had given me something else to think about and the journey back to prison wasn't an enjoyable experience. The assault orchestrated by Watson had set my thoughts back to the dark days of my youth and I thought I was on a merry go round playing the same scenario over and over again. The girl in my life was pregnant and I was miles away from home albeit this time not by choice.

I didn't know what to do but I had a decision I had to make.

Jessie had said in her letter that she wanted to visit to tell me about something, something I now knew was her pregnancy and I had three days to make up my mind whether I was finally going to see her. I still didn't want her waiting for me but the baby had put a diffcrent perspective on things.

We pulled up at the prison and I expected to return to the relative comfort of solitary but instead I was taken straight back to hell.

The anger began to return almost at once and I knew I could no longer get the sedative I needed to be able to control it. My weekly allowance was due and I spent it at once on cigarettes. In the past they had managed to chill me out a little but as I drew on the first one I felt my stress levels shooting up.

Badger noticed my anxiousness and tried his best to find out what was wrong. He knew about Dad's suicide but nothing about the baby and when I finally managed to tell him he muttered something I didn't quite hear and disappeared from our cell.

Twenty minutes later he was back.

I was lying on my bunk just staring blankly at the ceiling as Badger went to work rolling a few of his own cigarettes. When he had finished he lit one offering it to me after he had taken a draw from it. I took it from his hand mumbling my thanks and inhaled from the roll up without a second thought.

I noticed the change in taste immediately and looked at Badger in disbelief.

I was smoking a joint.

I knew drugs were rife on our wing and there were a few occasions when I'd been deliberately bumped into by one or two of the dealers asking if I wanted anything. I'd always refused politely saying I didn't smoke which at the time was true.

I was disappointed with Badger for forcing it onto me without my agreement and handed the joint back to him saying I didn't want it. He took a few steps backwards so I climbed down from my bunk with the intention of stubbing it out in the ashtray.

"It'll relax you," Badger said, "just try the one and if it doesn't help then don't have any more."

I looked at him with my hand hovering over the ashtray. He was serious in what he was saying about it being beneficial to me and I knew I needed something. I was scared about doing it though, the very thought of taking drugs had been something I had been against all my life. I associated it with junkies and desperate people, low life unemployed dropouts who hadn't got any hope of a future. People from the gutter, thieves and murderers. Yet, where was I? Slap bang in the middle of all of them.

What was wrong with just the one joint? What did I have to lose? It hadn't bothered me when the doctor prescribed sedatives when I was told that Dad had killed himself and what were they if not drugs!

I hesitated still wanting to stub the roll up out but then slowly brought it back towards my mouth. I looked at Badger and watched as he picked up another of the joints he'd made and lit that as well taking a huge toke into his lungs. He exhaled and the distinctive aroma enveloped me as I stood watching. I then did the same. In less than a minute both joints had been smoked and as I stubbed the remnants of mine out I got an overwhelming desire to laugh. I couldn't understand why, it wasn't as though anything was funny. I had been so full of trepidation as to what might happen to me I was totally unaware of any possible effects the drug might have. As it was I just looked back at Badger and carried on laughing. Maybe it was just relief that I wasn't seeing multi coloured flying elephants that made me smile. I was sure that the drug wasn't working and that was what was making me happy.

It wasn't teatime but Badger asked me if I was feeling hungry. I thought it a strange question but suddenly realised I was actually quite starving, a feeling I hadn't had in jail for quite a long time. My appetite over the weeks had diminished because of the quality of the food and it wasn't often my body craved replenishment. I had managed to acquire a bar of chocolate during my trip to Dad's funeral and I pulled it out of my pocket ripping the wrapper off and hurriedly devouring it. I caught a glimpse of Badger smiling.

"If you need another smoke..." Badger trailed off his sentence but I wasn't really listening. I was climbing back into my bunk to lie down. I felt relaxed as I lay there thankful that the cannabis hadn't had any affect on me, what did Badger know? Did he think he was a doctor or something?

I began thinking of Jessie again and smiled at the thought. I was going to be a father. The world was a wonderful place again and I knew it was time to talk to Jessie.

CHAPTER NINETEEN

I woke up from my dreams of Jessie as the teatime shout went up. Something wasn't quite right, my first thought should have been of something good but it wasn't. All I could think of was that bastard's penis in my mouth. I jumped out of bed and urged loudly into my bucket.

Fuck, what was wrong with me?

I was sure that I had been in a good mood before I'd fallen asleep. I tried to remember what I'd been doing. Dad's funeral...seeing Jessie pregnant...the joint. That was it, the joint. It had worked. The drug had done what Badger had said it would. My good feelings weren't of it not working but because it had. That was what it was meant to do.

"No...o...o" I yelled standing up and kicking my bucket across the cell floor spilling its contents.

Badger had already gone for tea and I was alone. I didn't leave the cell even though I was still starving. I just waited for Badger to come back.

"I need another one." I told him as he returned at six.

He looked at me and frowned asking me why.

"Because it took away the pain," I replied, "the mental pain."

"O.k," he said, "I'll do you one but if you're going to start smoking it you'll have to buy your own."

"I will, I will." I sounded desperate and Badger told me I'd have to wait a few minutes until the doors locked and then he would show me how to roll my own. He didn't want to be responsible for anything I chose to do in the future.

Ten minutes later Badger had retrieved his block of cannabis resin from where he had hidden it and was in the process of showing me how to roll my own spliff.

I watched mesmerised at the speed and skill he showed in making the joint mixing the brown scrapings of cannabis evenly with the tobacco. He expertly rolled the paper and its contents into a perfect cigarette shape pushing a cardboard filter into one end and twisting the other into a pointed taper ready for lighting. I couldn't even begin to think that I would ever be that good or that fast.

He offered me the joint and lit it as I put it between my lips. My eager anticipation had taken the bad thoughts out of my mind and I was relatively chilled before I'd taken my first puff.

"You owe me one...when you get sorted." Badger said as I exhaled and I knew I was in his debt.

All the time I was smoking I was relaxing and able to talk openly to Badger. I asked him where I could get my hands on my own cannabis.

My best bet happened to be from one of Dave's gang of friends, a guy called Johnny who was inside for dealing anyway. Badger thought it best to have a word with him first to let him know my intentions were honest and that I wasn't likely to grass him up. I wouldn't have dreamt of it, I'd learnt enough about Dave to realise that none of them were to be messed with.

I got sorted with my own lump of blow the following day. Badger was getting a bit pissed off with me constantly asking him to go and do the deal. On his return he warned me to go steady, it wasn't an answer to my problems but just a way of putting them out of my mind. He said I needed professional help and ought to have a word with the doctor to try and arrange counselling. I didn't agree and said I'd always sorted out my own problems my own way and this time wasn't going to be any different.

Badger shook his head as I grabbed what I was seeing as my cure and sat down at the small table to begin my first attempt at rolling a joint. I was proud of myself when I'd finished, it didn't look anything like it was supposed to but I'd managed to join it in all the right places. It took ages to smoke as I'd packed it with too much and too tightly but it still had the desired effect and I lay on my bed as the world passed me by. I laughed; it was definitely the way to make time go quickly.

The next couple of days were much the same and I was smoking at least five joints a day. Badger was concerned that I was doing too much and that if it continued at the rate it was then I was certain to get myself into debt. I wasn't interested in what he was telling me because I felt so good. I wished I'd discovered it years earlier then I wouldn't have ended up where I was.

I'd made up my mind to see Jessie if she turned up and I was delighted when an officer knocked on our door at three o'clock on visiting day to tell me that I had a visitor.

"Are you o.k?" were her concerned first words when I greeted her at the table. I must have given her a false impression of how I was feeling because of the way I looked. I had not long finished a joint when I was told that Jessie was waiting and the effects of that were still fresh. I wasn't exactly laughing but I felt as though I had the most ridiculous smile on my face and that would have appeared that I was either really pleased to see her or that I was having fun inside prison.

In a way I was terrified of seeing her, it had been a long time and although I had been determined not to speak to her ever again seeing her at Dad's funeral had brought back all my underlying feelings and the reality of her pregnancy had changed a lot inside my head. The thought of impending fatherhood scared the life out of me and I couldn't remember any part of my past where I had even thought about having children. There was the time with Alice when I had hoped her pregnancy was because of me but after finding out that it wasn't the thoughts of being a father never entered my head again.

It was my obvious first question because I needed confirmation from Jessie.

"Is it really mine?"

I said it with a smile on my face; I didn't want her to think that I imagined her to have been with someone else. I knew that she was going to wait for me whatever the outcome and anyway I hadn't been inside long enough for her to be so advanced.

Jessie smiled back and I knew I hadn't offended her.

"Yes!" she replied then almost immediately her smile vanished, her head dropped slightly and she spoke sadly.

"I wish you were out of here, I need you with

me...more than ever."

It was pointless her speaking like that, I was inside for a long time there was no getting away from it. Thoughts of the baby suddenly hit home. I was going to miss the birth. I was going to miss the early years. First words. First steps. First everything. I don't know what it was, whether the buzz of the cannabis was beginning to wear off or whether I was more screwed up than I thought but I shocked not only Jessie but myself as well as I blurted out something I didn't even know was in my mind.

"Get rid of it!"

CHAPTER TWENTY

The look of horror on Jessie's face matched my own disbelief in what I'd just said and we both sat there in shock, silent as we tried to come to terms with the words that had come out of my mouth. Words that I desperately wished I hadn't said. I couldn't imagine how me telling Jessie to abort our baby would feel to her but I did know that she was going to react.

She did, but not in the way I thought. I was expecting a verbal blast but instead I felt the full force of her hand as she slapped me hard across the face with as much strength as she could muster. My head jerked sideways and Jessie stood up ready to slap me again but she didn't get the chance as two of the officers on duty rushed across to grab hold of me and drag me out of the room.

"You bastard!" were the last words I heard as I was manhandled back to my cell.

"What the fuck have you been up to?" Badger asked as the guards left me lying in a heap on the cell floor.

"Fuck off!" I snapped back and climbed into my

bunk still shell shocked at the chaos I'd just caused.

An hour later I was with the governor in his office. A report of the incident had been handed to him and I had been called in to explain. He wanted to know if it was in any way connected to my father's death and whether I needed some sort of bereavement counselling. I explained as vaguely as I could that it was a personal matter and that I could deal with it on my own. The only counselling I needed right then was in the comfort of a joint.

For five days after that all I did was smoke dope and stay in my cell. I was pissing Badger off with my ignorance but I couldn't honestly give a fuck what he thought. My block of resin had all but run out and I needed more. I checked my money and could just about scrape together enough with my weekly allowance to buy some. The amount I was smoking was getting out of control but I needed it more and more to detach myself from the real world. I sought out Johnny and did the deal. He expressed his concern that I was doing too much but I told him to mind his own business and just come up with the goods when I wanted them. It didn't occur to me that I might be antagonising him with my attitude, I was still too naïve about the drug scene and what power a dealer could have if he thought I was getting too big for my boots.

I got even worse over the next few days and my cannabis ran out even quicker than I imagined it would. I needed more but I didn't have any money. I tried to cadge from Badger but he refused to let me have even one joint.

"It's your problem," he said, "sort it out your fucking self."

I didn't want to get into debt but I didn't have much choice. I saw Johnny and bought some on credit, I didn't realise it but I was then completely under his control.

Dave heard about my credit arrangement from Johnny and one morning he was waiting in the corridor as I was on my way to slopping out. He asked if he could have a quiet word in his cell and judging by the expression on his face I could hardly refuse. He still scared the shit out of me and even more so when he explained what would happen if I let my debt get out of hand. It was a reality check that I needed and for a while I cut down on my dope habit until I'd saved up enough to pay off what I owed.

It took two weeks to get myself straight with Johnny and as much as it was a relief not to have Dave's threats hanging over me it brought back all the mental torture I'd been trying to forget.

FADING LIGHT

I'd received a letter from Jessie telling me that she
wouldn't be in again and that she would be having
the baby no matter what I thought. She said that I
would always be the father and that she would
always be there for me but that it was up to me
whether there was any future for us. Although I
had been keeping them safe since I had been
inside I ripped up every letter she had ever sent.
I began suffering terrible mood swings, the lack of
dope reopening all my old wounds, wounds that
had also been reawakened thanks to the incident
in the toilets. I was thankful that Watson had
been removed from our wing but still lived in fear
that something similar was going to happen at
any time. I knew there were still incidents going
on between prisoners who consented to that sort
of practice but it still scared me rigid if I was ever
in the slopping out area with only a couple of
other prisoners around. I even resorted to
punching one fellow inmate full in the face when
he innocently put his hand on my shoulder.
It was time for Dave to have another quiet word.
Without going into details I tried to explain how I
couldn't cope without the amount of cannabis
that I needed, that it was the only thing that was
keeping me sane but the fact that I could no
longer afford the quantities I wanted was driving
me crazy. I begged for his help.

Dave listened quietly to my pleas and then told me to wait in my cell until he and Johnny paid a visit, he said he would bring something to help.

I felt calm as I waited alone. Badger had left the cell as soon as I returned, our friendship had deteriorated to the point of barely speaking and that suited me. I had been going to ask for a move to a single cell such was my need for solitude but I knew I wasn't going to be allowed that luxury, as it was the lack of communication with Badger seemed to be the next best thing.

As I sat on the edge of Badger's bed I wondered just what it was Dave would bring with him that could possibly help me. He said that Johnny would be with him and knowing that he was a dealer I knew it couldn't possibly be anything legal. I began hoping that he had some sort of arrangement with the prison doctor and could get hold of the sort of sedative that had helped me when Dad died. That would do the trick and I was sure that a bottle of pills wouldn't be as expensive as the amount I'd been spending on dope.

Forty minutes later Dave and Johnny appeared and I felt a rush of excitement surge through my body, I could feel an end to my torment was coming.

Dave stood by the cell door as Johnny entered and beckoned me over to the small table. I thought it was going to be a five second deal...hand me the pills and go.

How wrong I was.

Johnny reached into one of his pockets and pulling out a small bag and strangely a piece of foil and the plastic tube of a ballpoint pen. Out of the bag he took a couple of what looked like small rocks and placed them on the foil. Somewhat nervously he looked back towards Dave who just nodded. Johnny then reached into his pocket again and pulled out a lighter and a piece of paper that had been rolled to form a taper that he then proceeded to light. He brought the flame towards the foil and whatever it was he had placed on it. I watched intrigued, I didn't know what the hell was going on. It didn't take long for the rocks to melt and release a smoke that seemed to dance about in the air. Quickly Johnny grabbed the plastic tube and sucked in the dancing cloud. Then he passed the tube to me and told me to follow suit. I was shit scared but I did what I was told breathing the smoke deep into my lungs still completely oblivious to what I was actually inhaling.

CHAPTER TWENTY-ONE

I felt like someone had put a warm blanket around me I felt so good. There were a hundred people with me and they were all laughing, not in a bad way like taking the piss out of me but laughing with me. I was on stage again and the past had become reality once more. I was the centre of attention and I was loving every minute of it, telling joke after joke watching the reaction of the crowd as they too were having the time of their lives.

"Thank you and goodnight!" I heard myself saying before bowing and walking off into the waiting arms of Dad and Jessie. I hugged them both as tightly as I could a massive smile on my face. I felt something tugging me around the waist and I looked down to see a little boy desperate to be a part of the affectionate huddle.

The tugging continued and I gazed into his eyes seeing the urgency etched on his face. I was about to reach down to him to pick him up when his expression began to change. The features on his face began to alter. He was growing bigger and older and so rapidly. The tugging had turned to shaking and I was getting cold and scared. It wasn't a little boy any more it was a fully grown man and it seemed like he was attacking me. What was happening? I put up my hands to defend myself and the shaking stopped. I could hear voices, my assailant was trying to speak to me and I realised I knew him. I sat bolt upright in my bunk and threw up straight into the face of Badger.

His reaction was understandable. He grabbed me with both hands and pulled me off the bed letting me fall to the ground, I did nothing to stop him I was still adjusting to the fact that what I'd just experienced in my mind was just a dream and nothing like the reality I thought it was.

"You stupid bastard," I heard him yell, "what the fuck do you think you're doing?"

I hadn't got any idea what he was talking about and stared blankly at him from where I lay.

He reached out towards the table and picked up the piece of foil that Johnny had left behind thrusting it into my face.

"Heroin?"

At first the word didn't register, I began looking around the cell for all the people that had been there minutes before. Where was Dad, Jessie and the little boy. More to the point where was I?

"Heroin?"

Badger was asking the question again and that time it hit home. I was coming back to the real world. Heroin. It was a word that had always struck fear into me, other drugs like cannabis, LSD even cocaine didn't seem to have the fear factor that a word like heroin had. It was the word of addicts, filth and desperation. It was the word of overdose and death, yet for all that it wasn't what I'd just experienced. If heroin was so bad then why had I just had such a feeling of elation? I couldn't think of a time when I'd had such a wonderful sense of well-being. Badger could say what the fuck he liked. He could lecture me about the bad side of heroin as much as he wanted, I'd heard all about it before and it had truly scared me but what he couldn't do was tell me anything about its good side, the good side that I'd just seen. I'd had a fix of this supposedly evil drug yet I'd felt totally exhilarated and there was no way that could be a bad thing. I was back in the real world and yet I hated it even more as it had ruined the excitement I'd just been woken up from. I wanted to go back and I couldn't wait until I'd caught up with Johnny again.

CHAPTER TWENTY-TWO

Badger tried as hard as he could to convince me of the pitfalls of taking a drug like heroin but in my mind he didn't have an argument, no case for the prosecution I cynically laughed, heroin the accused was definitely not guilty he was free to do as he pleased.

The next morning came soon enough and I was out through the door almost as soon as the locking device was activated to open. I was so keen to get to Johnny that I virtually pushed my way into his cell. He wasn't as pleased to see me as I was him but it didn't bother me, I was interested in only one thing.

Johnny slammed the door behind me and fixed me with an icy glare.

"Do you know how fucking dangerous it is to deal in here?" he hissed into my face, "if we do this then we do it my way."

He was right. I was being an idiot. What was I thinking just bounding in like I was after a bag of sweets from the local shop? Yet again my naivety of the criminal world was blatantly obvious. I was like a flashing beacon to every screw in the place.

For a moment I was glad we weren't dealing on the outside as Johnny seemed the type who wouldn't think twice about putting a blade to my throat.

"Sorry." I mumbled.

Johnny opened the door telling me to join him and Dave in the exercise yard after breakfast making it clear that it wasn't a game but deadly serious, I was no longer messing about with a bit of blow I was entering the dark side of prison life and getting caught would put years on my sentence.

The deal was done as arranged; I wandered around the yard a few times until I was beckoned over by Dave where in a huddle the heroin was slipped swiftly into my pocket. I didn't realise I'd been passed the drug until the huddle broke up and Dave told me to be on my way. The heroin this time was in powder form as it was apparently easier to conceal than the rocks that Johnny had brought with him the first time and I felt an expectant warmth envelop me as I clenched my fist around it. I was desperate to get my second fix to remind myself of just how good it felt but I didn't feel it was right to rush off straight away. After my mistake in seeking out Johnny earlier that morning I didn't want to draw any attention to myself so I just kept walking around the yard until the exercise period was over.

Dave joined me at one point to discuss payment.

"There's enough for twenty hits there and it will work out cheaper than dope...if you're sensible."

Back in my cell it wasn't long before the sweet smell of the burning heroin filled the air and I was inhaling the black dancing dragon hungrily. I chased the smoke as it swirled around desperate not to lose any of the precious drug. I'd been quite liberal with the amount of powder I had put on the piece of foil; I wanted to make sure that there was enough of it to take me back to where I had been the day before.

Badger had been angry when he saw me setting up my fix but there was nothing he could do about it. If he created a scene then that would have resulted in a cell search, which in turn would have unearthed his stash of cannabis, and I was sure he didn't want a longer sentence than he already had. I offered him a chance to chase the dragon with me but he just turned his back without a word. I screwed up the foil when I'd finished and tossed it into my bucket, I could get rid of the evidence the following morning.

The music played loudly as I climbed the stairs pushing through the double door entrance to Mulvey's club. I stood there for a moment surveying the scene, the ambience enveloping me like an opening night had done so many times before. Every face in the crowd appeared to be of someone I'd met in the past, everyone except those who had sought to do me harm. It was like a surprise birthday party and everybody was so pleased to see me, I was being greeted like a long lost friend. I walked towards them shaking hands, hugging, kissing making my way through the crowd and towards the bar where Mulvey was waiting beaming broadly in the way only he could. He was clutching a bottle of my favourite whisky and pointing towards the stage. My eyes followed his directing finger and there sat side by side were two of the most beautiful people in the world...Alice and my Mum. They looked so happy and so alive. I didn't wait for a drink I just rushed towards the stage and flung my arms around the pair of them. I was crying and so were they. This was a perfect moment...we were all back together once again.

FADING LIGHT

CHAPTER TWENTY-THREE

That was my life for the next ten days, I'd found a new best friend and once again it wasn't a real person. In the early days after I first left home the holiday campsite became a true friend to me because it was somewhere I distanced myself from the emotional trauma in my life and now I'd found another escape from everything...heroin.

I was doing two hits a day, mid morning and early evening. I cut down on the amount I was burning after my first attempt because it was a long time before I came back to the real world and although that was the point of taking the drug in the first place I didn't like the thought that I could quite easily have overdosed.

I missed quite a few meals because of my habit and it was making me lose weight quite rapidly. Badger was concerned at how ill I was looking but it didn't matter to me what I looked like on the outside because on the inside I was feeling the best I had since being locked up.

The personal standards I'd had prior to being convicted had all but disappeared. I didn't wash, shave or even clean my teeth. Whatever food I did manage to eat mainly came out as diarrhoea but I didn't care; to me it made slopping out easier.

I'd paid Johnny for my first supply of heroin and after receiving my allowance for the following week I approached him for some more. I didn't want to run out before he could provide me with what I needed. Surprisingly Johnny said I could pay him later and I assumed that for some reason I had regained his trust.

I got back to my cell and shoved my money under my pillow before hiding my newly received package. I felt really good so went outside to the exercise yard to get some fresh air before my mid morning fix. I was sat on one of the benches when Dave came and sat next to me.

He was abrupt with what he wanted...the money for the drugs.

He wasn't happy that Johnny had let me go without paying up front. Money first drugs later was his way of doing business after the first deal, Johnny knew better than giving credit on heroin without asking him first. I assured him that I had the money and rushed off to get it.

It wasn't where I'd left it.

I searched frantically, stripping my bed bare; it wasn't anywhere to be found. I turned the whole cell upside down even going through Badger's stuff, there was still no sign of my money but even worse than that...my heroin had gone too.

I didn't know what to do; I was in a panic. What was Dave going to say when I told him I couldn't pay? I was sure I could get him to agree to let me have some on credit but that wasn't the point, what was he going to say when I told him that I wanted some more heroin and that I couldn't pay for that either? Shit. I couldn't let him know, I had to try and find out who had robbed me. There was one obvious culprit. Badger. He had been totally against me using smack so it had to be him. He must have seen where I had hidden it and waited until he was sure he could steal it without me knowing. I had to find him and fast.

I hadn't noticed him in the exercise yard but having left Dave there that was the last place I was going to look. There weren't many other places he could be, if we weren't outside we were meant to return to our cells. Maybe he was in the toilets. I was about to head there when Badger walked into the cell.

"You thieving bastard!" I shouted lunging towards him sending my fist crashing into his jaw. He staggered back out into the corridor and I followed pulling back my fist ready to strike him again. He didn't have a chance to defend himself as my knuckles made contact with his nose. I heard the bone crack as blood spurted over his face and across my hand.

"Stop." I heard him say but it was too late for that, I was intent on teaching him a lesson, a lesson he would learn from.

"Where the fuck is it?" I snarled into his ear as I held him in a headlock. He started to choke as he inhaled his own blood.

"Where the fuck is it?" I demanded again relaxing my grip slightly giving him the opportunity to reply.

He didn't. Instead he pushed with all his remaining strength taking me by surprise as we both ended up in a heap back inside our cell.

The situation had reversed, Badger now had the advantage pinning me to the floor with his weight. With his free hands he punched me repeatedly in the face and upper body. It hurt. I wasn't in any way fit enough to be fighting. In such a short space of time my body had wasted away and I was barely over nine stone thanks to the lack of food and the toll the drugs had inflicted. I went limp and didn't make any effort to fight back.

Badger must have realised I wasn't retaliating and his punches became softer and less frequent until he finally stopped. I was still seething inside and I tried to speak but my swollen mouth made it difficult and the words came out slurred. I hadn't had an answer from Badger about my heroin and

I didn't get one at least not verbally. I watched as he reached into his pocket and pulled out a handful of notes dropping them onto me as he stood up.

"I don't want my fucking money back, I want my smack...I need a fucking fix."

I was almost crying in desperation, I had temporarily forgotten about Dave even though I now had the means to pay him off, I just wanted the sanctuary that heroin offered me to be away from everything and everyone, to be alone, to be out of the miserable fucked up world I had the misfortune to be part of.

"Please," I begged Badger, "give it back."

"I can't, I've sold it, what do you think the money's for?"

Sold it? What was he saying? He'd stolen my drugs just to sell? What the fuck for? Why did he need money it wasn't as though he wanted to buy a new television or anything.

"You need help," he continued, "look at the mess you're in. I'm doing what's best for you."

I tried to stand up, I wanted to fight him again to show him what sort of a mess I was in but I was too weak and collapsed back down to the floor. My body may have not been in any state to tackle Badger but my mind was still active. I needed drugs and I had money, more than I owed Dave by the look of it and possibly enough to buy some more. Badger was stupid if he thought that stealing my heroin would put an instant end to my habit; there was no way I would give up my friend that easily.

I lay there for a moment contemplating my next move, I had to get back to Dave with his money before the cell doors were locked and that was due to happen any minute. I thought about cleaning my bloodied face but decided against it hoping that my injuries and explanation would make Dave view Badger in a different light, that he would see that my loss was in no way my fault. I sat up and grabbed the money that Badger had dropped on the floor counting it carefully to make sure that I had enough to fund my next deal. I sighed with relief when the total reached the amount I had hoped for.

I looked across at Badger who was tidying up his ransacked belongings, blood was still pouring from his broken nose but I felt no sympathy for him in fact there was still a score to be settled. Whether it was me or Dave that settled it didn't matter Badger was going to get what was coming.

I thrust my wad of notes into my pocket and snarled threateningly into Badger's ear once more.

"Touch my fucking drugs EVER again and

you'll fucking regret it."
I didn't wait for a reply as I hurried out of the cell to try and catch up with Dave fearful that he might think I wasn't coming back. It didn't bear thinking about how that would appear to someone as prone to violence as he was; I wasn't ready for another fight.

With good reason Dave didn't look too pleased when he saw me, I'd been gone over half an hour to do something that should have taken two minutes.

"Sorry Dave," I said as apologetically as I could, "I had a bit of a problem."

Dave wasn't interested, even though he couldn't help but see my blood splattered face he just wanted his money. I tried to explain what had happened but Dave just took the cash that I was holding out to him and started to walk away.

"I need some more smack." I shouted a little too loudly and instantly regretted it as Dave stopped in his tracks before turning and looking at me menacingly.

"What's your fucking problem?" he growled and I felt whatever colour I had left drain from my face.

I was petrified but I couldn't let it show, I didn't want to upset him any further than I already had.

"I need some more heroin, Badger stole and

sold everything I had."

Dave's reaction wasn't pleasant and he said something I wasn't expecting.

"Are you fucking stupid? This isn't a fucking game we're playing I'm not running a corner shop, there...is...no...more..."

Dave said the last four words slowly to make a point but it was lost on me, what he was actually saying didn't register and I grabbed him by the shoulder.

"I need a fix...NOW"

Dave didn't say another word he just reached up and removed my hand before punching me hard in the stomach. I doubled up in agony dropping to my knees. A split second later I felt the full force of his boot connect under my chin.

CHAPTER TWENTY-FOUR

My jaw had been broken thanks to Dave's vicious assault and by the time I came out of the prison hospital Badger, Dave and Johnny had all gone.
Badger had unwittingly started a clean up campaign by the governor to rid our wing of its ever increasing drug culture and the violence that was quite often associated with it. I never got to learn the full story but I heard that Badger, even though he was a cannabis user, had started to grass everybody up. Maybe he saw what my introduction to heroin had done to me and was doing it as some sort of misguided charitable good deed but what did he really know about my situation. He didn't know the whole truth of why I was inside in the first place nor did he know the full facts of what happened when Watson arrived at the prison. I didn't ask for his help and I certainly didn't want it.
I spent six weeks in hospital with my jaw wired and it was hell. The doctors could tell I'd been doing heroin for a while and the withdrawal from it was quite horrific. Despite being given methadone I went through every emotion possible

except happiness and I really wanted my life to end there and then. If I had had the means to do it I know for certain that I would have.

The involuntary muscle spasms, the cold turkey goose bumps and all the other reactions to my body I could cope with because of the methadone but it was the dreams that were almost impossible to deal with. All the reasons for starting drugs in the first place returned to the forefront of my mind and I knew that whatever detox programme they put me on would never work. They could get the drugs out of my system easily and successfully but they couldn't erase the mental pain that was virtually branded on my mind. I could see it and feel it twenty four hours a day and no amount of counselling would ever take it away. I needed heroin like never before and I was determined to score as soon as I was back on the wing.

Dave's attack was witnessed by a few guards and he was hauled off to solitary almost immediately. He was eventually put on an assault charge and removed to a higher security prison, trouble was he'd left a few of his friends behind and I was wary of how they were going to react to me once I was back amongst them.

I missed the clean up campaign as the governor swept through the wing showing no tolerance to any criminal activity. Every single cell was subject to random searches in his effort to rid his prison of drugs.

Johnny was busted the same day Dave put me in hospital and when I finally heard about it I was under no illusions that my desire to do heroin again was going to be difficult to put into practice. I needed to find a new dealer but there seemed to be a new level of animosity towards me. I guessed it either had something to do with loyalty to Dave and Johnny or else they had been threatened. I began to regret that I hadn't mingled with other prisoners as much as I should have done and once again I began to feel totally alone.

Thankfully on my release from hospital I had been put in a single cell and judging by the bad feeling amongst the other prisoners it seemed a perfect solution to my predicament. I couldn't imagine the tension that would have existed if I'd been forced to share a cell with any of Dave's group of friends.

I hated the feeling of isolation that I had and although I welcomed the hours of solitude alone in my cell it was at mealtimes that the magnitude of bitterness towards me really hit home. I sat by no one and no one sat by me. I was jostled and spat on in the queue for food and more often than not waited until I was the last one to be served. My anger was welling up inside and I was sorely tempted to let my frustrations loose on somebody...anybody.

The cell searches had all but stopped by the time I was returned to the wing, the governor probably thought that by doing away with people like Dave and Johnny would eradicate the problem but as is always the case with people in authority they assume they have all the answers. The good news for people like me though was that in the criminal world when a man like Dave was removed there was always someone else ready and willing to take their place, they would just be biding their time until it was safe enough to start dealing again.

Despite my lack of involvement with everyone else I had to keep my eyes and ears open so I could spot just who the dealers were. I was desperate for some sort of activity on the drugs front and I thought that if I was to find someone who was willing to deal with me then I would probably have to pay over the odds, a sort of bribe, to make it worth their while. I had been lucky in one respect that whilst in hospital and being given methadone I hadn't had to pay for the real stuff and over the course of six weeks my allowance had built up into a decent sum of money and nothing meant more to a prospective dealer than the sight of ready cash.

The single cell I had been allocated was in the

noisiest part of the wing and the next two nights were almost intolerable, music blasted out all night long and I had the impression that the inmates who occupied the single cells were using music as a substitute for companionship. I was glad to have no one to talk to but that obviously didn't appeal to everyone and the solitude I had been looking forward to just didn't happen. I wasn't in a position to complain about it either as my standing with the rest of the wing was at an all time low. I knew I had to accept it but I couldn't, it irritated me beyond belief and the desire to score again grew stronger and stronger.

I blamed the prison authorities for stopping giving me methadone the moment I was returned to the wing and I blamed myself for coping with the effects of withdrawal so easily. I'd assumed that it would only be a few hours before I hit the drugs trail on my release and I hadn't banked on the clean up campaign.

I needed something desperately and I thought of faking the symptoms of 'cold turkey' on the half chance that I might be given methadone again.

I didn't need to.

On the third morning back after my jaw had healed I spotted what I thought was a deal being done in the exercise yard. With the removal of Badger, Dave and Johnny a new group of prisoners had arrived to take their place and it was one of them that had seemed to me to have slipped a package to someone I knew smoked cannabis. It was the move I had been waiting for and I knew if I was to regain my sanity I had no choice but to make my desires known. I briefly thought about blackmail and using what I'd seen as a threat but decided against it. I felt that most of the inmates hated me and that would make things worse for myself. I needed to be respected as Dave was not hated but what could I do? I was still barely over nine stone and didn't have the physical presence to strike fear into anybody. What was there about me that anyone could possibly like me for? I tried to think back to who I was before I ended up inside but couldn't. That was it; I hadn't got any idea who I was any more. I'd been inside for less than six months and I'd turned into a nobody, surely that wasn't long enough to forget myself? Maybe it was the drugs that had completely fucked my brain and I was becoming not just a junkie but a zombie as well.

I racked my brain, shouting at myself, screaming inside...who the fuck am I?...who the fuck am I? WHO THE FUCK AM I?

I ran my fingers through my unkempt hair grabbing a tight hold of it and pulling hard until it hurt. I scraped my fingernails down my face breaking the skin until thin traces of blood appeared. I didn't care who was looking at me, no one else existed, I was alone in the world and I started laughing...hysterically.

The more I laughed the more it triggered memories from my past, a feeling of something I recognised. I could make out images as I sat there laughing, a figure on a stage, a backdrop with a name on it, a name that slowly became clearer and clearer. Roo Reynolds...it spelt out and I could hear the laughter only it wasn't me any more it was too loud for that...I was looking away from the stage ...hundreds of people...they were laughing...laughing at me...Roo Reynolds. I'm Roo Reynolds...shit I'm Roo Reynolds.

It was like a huge cloud had been lifted and I was fully aware of who I was. For some reason someone was telling me how I could gain everyone's respect again. I just had to be myself...it was that simple. I was a real person before I ended up in prison and I would be a real person when I left so why shouldn't I be a real person while I was inside?

I knew I now had the means to become everyone's friend; it was something I should have done the moment I arrived. I was Roo Reynolds, comedian, entertainer. What was it about laughter being the best medicine? I was about to find out and if it earned me respect and the opportunity to reacquaint myself with my old friend heroin again then it was something I was going to use.

I went back to my cell in a somewhat reflective mood. I felt different and it was difficult to explain to myself just what it was. I'd heard people say that they'd seen the light in relation to situations that they had found themselves in but whether the experience I'd been through was me seeing the light was doubtful. I'd quite honestly felt I was going mad and if my finding myself or just remembering who I was, was in any way spiritual then that was bullshit, in my mind I'd just come up with a way of getting a much needed fix.

CHAPTER TWENTY-FIVE

It was the most enjoyable hit I had ever had although that was probably more to do with the sense of relief I felt when the relatively instant sensation careered around my body. It was the best feeling in the world and mingled with the reintroduction in my mind of one of the best periods of my life I felt as though I was in heaven. I had missed that feeling so much whilst I'd been in hospital and I couldn't understand how I'd coped as well as I had but that didn't matter any more...I was back where I wanted to be.

The abrupt rush as the drug took hold of me made me collapse and I think it was the realisation that I'd ended up on my bed that brought the memories of Alice's sixteenth birthday into my head. I remembered the pride I felt as she asked me to be her first on reaching the age of consent and all I could do was reminisce about lying in her arms. In my mind we made love over and over again, the warmth of her body as we lay entwined felt so real and I never ever wanted to be away from that.

I wanted to tell the whole world just how heroin

was making me feel...to me it was quite literally a wonder drug and that everyone should experience at least once the high elation that it gave.

The deal had been done earlier in the evening and I had planned it pretty well like a military manoeuvre. The way I felt after rediscovering myself meant that there was no way I was going to be turned down by anyone and what made it easier for me was the fact that the person I thought had started to deal was a new inmate and chances were he didn't know about my brush with Dave and Johnny. I was confident that my sought after satisfaction was to fulfilled.

I hung around outside the dining hall until my intended new supplier appeared and then joined the queue directly behind him.

"Are you dealing?" I whispered in his ear making sure no one else could hear. He didn't answer or even acknowledge my existence so I put my plan into action as if I was trying to wake up an unresponsive audience. I spilled out about half a dozen one-line jokes, the sort of sarcastic humour that most people found hard not to smirk at. I still didn't get a response at least not from my prospective dealer but a couple of others in the queue reacted with a smile. I could feel I was onto a winner and once again wished I'd made an effort sooner. I tried a couple of jokes that had always gone down well in the past and this time got a couple of laughs, I was on a roll and launched myself into the start of a routine carrying it on until we'd each received our food. I joined my target and a few others at one of the tables convinced that I wouldn't be shunned and started to eat my food.

One by one they introduced themselves and I felt that my acceptance into their lives was close. I tried to start a conversation with them intermittently inserting a few more jokes and got a few that I hadn't heard before in return. Glancing around the room I noticed that as always I was the object of attention but whereas in the past it was mainly done to intimidate me this time everyone seemed to be trying to listen to what I was saying. It was a sign of encouragement and I deliberately raised my voice. The normal hubbub subsided and I had a captive audience. I couldn't resist and I had to seize the opportunity by standing up and going into a full routine, the more I got into it the more I began to remember and subsequently enjoy. The buzz I was getting was the way I wanted everyone to feel and if I could manage that then I was clear in my mind that I would be able to do away with the hostility that had built up.

I stood up for about ten minutes not wanting to

push it any further, I didn't want to get on any
ones nerves but afterwards as I sat down I heard a
couple of claps which slowly increased into what
was polite applause. I wasn't expecting anything
like that but it showed that I was beginning to get
close to the approval I sought. Maybe the fact that
Dave wasn't around any longer dictating what
went on in prison made them realise they were
free to do their own thing or maybe the
availability of drugs again made what Badger had
done seem irrelevant. I had come to realise that in
the drugs world the only thing that mattered was
the drug itself and that applied to me as well
because that was my only purpose in doing what I
was doing. I knew I still had a long stretch in front
of me and none of the people on my wing were
likely to be friends of mine in the outside world
but while I was inside I was going to use them for
my own benefit. Humour was to be my weapon
and they were going to be my victims; it wouldn't
be long before I was in complete control of the
wing and nothing was going down unless I said
so.

I smiled to myself at the thought and that of my
earlier prediction that someone would take Dave's
mantle. I hadn't even contemplated that it might
be me but then why not? Why shouldn't it be me?
Why should it have to be someone as violent as

FADING LIGHT

Dave? Why couldn't someone get the same respect that Dave got but without the necessary force that he used? It was something for me to ponder over the coming weeks and although my primary aim was just to get my supply of heroin with my first method of attack being humour I was still likely to do it by any means that I possibly could.

Nothing untoward happened over the next three weeks and the wing seemed to be turning into a place of mellow tranquillity. I got hold of my supply of smack on a regular basis from my new dealer friend, Frankie, and the ease of that, coupled with the unlikely bonding of everyone, made my mental anguish rapidly disappear.

Jessie no longer existed in my thoughts even when I wasn't under the influence of smack she had been banished to the recesses of my mind. I had the occasional lapse when I was in my cell and had come out of a hit sooner than I'd wanted but for the main part everything was peaceful and that was how I wanted it to remain.

Unfortunately I hadn't made allowances for a particular trait that affects far too many people...the trait of jealousy. I don't know whether it was because people were becoming jealous of me because of my increasing popularity and leadership...I had become a sort of small time Mr.

Big...or they were jealous of Frankie being the only dealer that anybody bought anything off.

As always there was a reasonably swift turnover of prisoners and a couple of lifer's were relocated to our wing. They didn't look the type that could be won over by the regime that I seemed to have inherited. Humour wasn't going to work on them, they didn't look as though they had ever smiled in their lives and it wasn't long before they made it clear that they wanted a piece of the action. For the first time since Dave and Johnny had been removed I felt fearful even though I had a close group of friends who wouldn't have thought twice about backing me up had anything got out of hand. Trouble was they got to Frankie first and subsequently dealt with me in a less than subtle way. Brutality had returned to the wing and nobody experienced it quite the way I did.

Frankie's cache of heroin from the outside world was of a particularly good quality and always gave me a far better hit than anything Johnny had ever dealt and I think it was because of that that I trusted Frankie implicitly. I took my new supply from him early one evening and like a kid with a new toy rushed back excitedly to try it out, inhaling the fumes deep into my lungs.

I ended up losing three days of my life.

CHAPTER TWENTY-SIX

My brush with death had a drastic affect on my life. Overdosing on heroin that was so pure it should have killed me wasn't just a wake up call, it felt as though I had drawn the curtains on my very existence. The governor had gone absolutely ballistic and it was something that he couldn't keep out of the press. His belief that he had overcome all the problems with drugs in his prison had been dramatically shattered. Each prisoner in turn was summoned to see him in a bid to find out what happened. The papers made a meal of it asking questions about the state of the prison service and how a former celebrity like myself could end up overdosing on heroin having only been inside for such a short period of time. The tabloids created such a stink about the whole episode that an official enquiry was set up which resulted in the governor being made a scapegoat and he eventually lost his job.

I was inundated with letters from the public most of which offered support urging me to get help and treatment and it was the content of those letters that made me realise for the first time that

I was a drug addict.

Jessie wrote too, a long gushing letter about how she felt and that I was a much better person than the one I was turning into. She blamed herself for putting too much pressure on me instead of giving me the support she felt I desperately needed. She begged me, for the sake of our unborn child, to demand the necessary detox and counselling programme that was available.

I didn't need to search it out because it came looking for me or rather the new governor did. He offered me untold help with everything and although I eventually accepted his offer I couldn't help but feel he was just using me, he wanted me to be a success story, someone who could overcome all my personal problems and be rehabilitated not only in prison but eventually back into society. I just listened, I was willing to give it a try but I still had a hell of a long time until I was anywhere near the end of my sentence and with too many incidents from my past likely to be relived I wasn't convinced that I wouldn't at some point suffer a relapse.

Detox wasn't good. I'd had a brief introduction after Dave broke my jaw but I only got through it because I knew that I'd be back on heroin as soon as I was back on the wing. This time it was a whole lot worse. Maybe it was the realisation that heroin wouldn't be there for me afterwards or maybe it was the recurrence of the nightmares that made me react the way I did...I didn't know...I just felt I was going through yet another bad patch in my life.

The counselling that went with the territory of detox was no better and in some ways even more painful than my experience with withdrawal. I was told right from the start that unless I opened up fully and confided in someone then I would never be fully cured. I wasn't sure whether I could go through the ordeal of talking to anyone, I had reached the point in my life where I hadn't needed to and I argued with the do-gooders, social workers, psychiatrists, counsellors, whoever the fuck they made me talk to until I was blue in the face that there was absolutely nothing they could do that would make me relinquish my personal hell. I couldn't see what it was likely to achieve, far better that it was confined to the past. Session after session they tried to drag everything out of me but what they couldn't see was they were pushing me too hard. My mind was in utter turmoil and it wasn't doing me any good at all. I stopped eating, couldn't sleep and above all I needed a fix. Why the fuck couldn't they see they were doing more harm than good? I was a hopeless case, a lost cause but they wouldn't give in. They said they could see it in me that I wanted to put an end to my pain and they were right because after one soul searching session I felt I couldn't take any more and fled back to my cell where I hacked at my wrists with a tooth brush that I managed to snap in half.

Once more I was in hospital on the edge of my life and for what? Because people thought they should know what my problems were? That they had a God given right to cure me? What was he going to do, open up his fucking pearly gates so he could kiss their arses instead of them forever kissing his? 'Welcome my children, you are truly the saviours of the lost soul' Well I didn't give a shit, this was one soul they weren't going to save and if I had a choice I would prefer to be banished to hell.

Without my knowledge or consent Jessie was informed of my attempt at suicide and a visit had been arranged with her that I was unaware of until I actually walked in the room. I thought I was going to another pointless meeting and to say I was shocked when I saw her was an understatement. I had forgotten just what she looked like such was the destruction of the happier side of my memory. I had spent so much time dredging up the murkiness of the past to the point that I felt I had never experienced anything even remotely worthwhile to remember. For some reason the only effect the counselling seemed to be have on me was to put negative thoughts in my mind or maybe that was just my defensive mechanism kicking into play.

It must have been the sight of her and her condition that the mess I was in finally hit home. Jessie was heavily pregnant and I guessed the birth was imminent...I hadn't got a clue...I had lost all recognition of time. To me it seemed only hours since I had been telling her to get rid of it.

I broke down, far worse than at any time in my life yet in a way it was a sense of relief, a sign that despite everything I had a future. A part of me that was positive actually existed.

CHAPTER TWENTY-SEVEN

"Give me your hand."
Jessie's first words were spoken softly and my uncertainty as to what she meant was noticed. I made to pull away as she reached for my hand, I think I was scared of how I might feel touching her again, but she grabbed hold of me anyway. She drew me towards her and placed my palm against her stomach.
"Can you feel that?" she asked, "it's our baby."
I felt something push at my hand and although I tried to move Jessie held me firmly.
"It's o.k." she instructed, "you can't harm it."
I didn't know what to say or how to react, words were forming in my head but I was terrified to say them. In less than five minutes Jessie had once again turned my whole world upside down. I'd deliberately turned my back on her so many times in an effort to make her realise she should have a life without me but she wouldn't go.
"Would you still be here if you weren't pregnant?" I asked her.
It was a cold question but one that I needed an answer to, I had to get clear in my head whether

she was there to help me as a person or whether she was just there because I was the father of her child.

I looked towards the ceiling; I couldn't face looking into her eyes as she answered.

"You know me better than that Roo."

She was right; I did know her better than that. The fact that she was there at all told me so. I'd told her to get rid of the baby, something no woman wants their partner ever to say to them yet by being there she had shown she had forgiven me for that callous act. In the short time I had known her before stabbing Tom I'd been struck by her honesty so when she said she was there for me I had to believe her, she wasn't old enough to have learnt the cynicism of telling lies to mask the truth.

She tried to put her arms around me, I assumed in an effort to show she was telling the truth, but as much as I wanted to respond I felt it was a little too early for me to show such emotion. Maybe when it was time for her to leave and I felt a little bit more comfortable in her company then I could respond in the right way but at that moment I just couldn't. I felt guilty about too many things that I'd said and done to her and I needed to apologise for them.

We sat down in the two chairs that were set in

front of the desk that my counsellor usually sat at. A prison officer was present all the time which made it difficult for us to talk about certain things but in a way it was a good thing as it meant Jessie wouldn't be telling me every couple of minutes that she loved me. I didn't want that, I didn't feel as though I deserved her love.

I wanted to talk about the situation at home, how she was and how what I had done was affecting everybody. I wanted to know about Tom and Dean and how they were treating her but I couldn't, I didn't trust our guard not to be listening. Instead we just talked about how I was going to go about my rehabilitation and what choices were open to me. Jessie had brought with her lots of leaflets explaining what could be done but I told her that I'd done all the things they suggested and none of them had worked.

"If I was on the outside then maybe it would work but it's difficult in here. You can't understand the loneliness and isolation of being banged up in a cell for so long every day."

"Then let me help you...write to me, call me, let me visit you. You have to get through this."

Yet again Jessie was right, she was telling me that she was someone I could open up to, that anything I told her would go no further. Maybe she was the one person I'd been looking for since the night of my sixteenth birthday, maybe finally she would be the one person I could actually tell. People like Tom and Watson and all the others that were there that night all knew but, as I was just beginning to realise, the counsellors were right...I needed to get it off my chest. Letters and phone calls were no good though, letters were always read before they were posted and phone calls were overheard. My only option was visiting day and being every fortnight I felt that they were too far apart.

"Maybe I could ask if you could sit in on a few of our meetings." I suggested to Jessie.

"If it works, I'll do anything to help you."

I got through the rest of the day quite easily thanks to Jessie, having her waiting on the outside was from then on going to be the main focus of my attention and I promised her before she left that I would keep on with the counselling and make more of an effort to be receptive to their methods.

I returned to the wing and back to a shared cell. I was told it was being done as companionship for me to help in my rehabilitation but I just assumed it was so somebody was there to keep an eye on me.

For the first time in ages I lay in bed that night not wanting drugs to take away the pain, I was high enough on thoughts of Jessie. I wanted to repay her faith, I wanted to share our baby and more than anything I wanted to be happy.

CHAPTER TWENTY-EIGHT

Occupying my mind was one of the main remedies taught me by one of my counsellors and although the first couple of days were spent thinking of Jessie I still needed something else.

I'd laughed it off as a joke before but when it was suggested again it didn't come across as such a bad idea. I joined the prison library and it was an absolute godsend. I hadn't been much of a reader at any point in my life, I'd always been too busy, but I quickly realised I had been missing out on so much. I read anything at first and found myself getting so engrossed that time passed quickly. Days flashed by so fast that I barely had time to think.

Jessie was hoping to visit eight days after our unexpected meeting but it was due to coincide at a time she was likely to give birth so when I got to the visiting room and saw not Jessie but Mary waiting for me I was elated and disappointed at the same time.

"Jessie's gone into labour," Mary told me, "but she wanted someone to be here to see you."

My disappointment at not seeing Jessie was short

lived because the birth was now only a matter of hours away. I was as excited as any expectant parent could be although I felt a tinge of sadness that I couldn't be present at the birth. Still, I'd been given an opportunity to find out just how Jessie was coping with everything and a chance to discover just what had happened since I'd been locked up. Even though I'd wanted to I didn't get the chance to speak to Mary before I'd been arrested and I had no knowledge about how she and Mikey had reacted and dealt with the situation I'd caused. I started with Jessie.

"How is she?"

"Happier now she's talking to you. You nearly destroyed that girl, she was in such a bad way."

I should have expected it, Mary wasn't happy with what I'd put Jessie through but I was a bit confused. As far as I could remember Mary didn't even know Jessie.

"How?" I asked, a frown creasing my brow.

"She looked after your Dad, lived with him after you got arrested. She tried to protect him from what Dean was doing."

"I didn't know..."

"She found him...can you imagine how that must have felt seeing him on the end of a rope?"

I couldn't, I tried to picture it but pictures don't always relay the true horror of a situation like that. I thought back to when she told me that she had witnessed Alice being pushed down the stairs by her father and how she wouldn't speak to anybody at all after that. I felt sick that I'd tried to kill myself without any thought of what that could have done to Jessie. All the death and destruction in her life was completely and totally down to me. I wanted to walk out of the room there and then but I needed to know more, I needed to know about Mary, Mikey, Dean, Mulvey and more than ever I needed to know about Tom. Whatever I felt about me being the cause of heartache for Jessie the true source for everybody's pain was the bastard who was still walking free.

"I'm sorry," I said and I genuinely meant it, "I didn't know Dad would kill himself. I thought by rejecting Jessie it would give her a better life...one away from me."

"You're so lucky to have her, remember that."

"Where's she living now?"

I was concerned because I thought that maybe she had returned home and I didn't want her bringing up our child in that sort of environment. What if Tom knew it was mine? I couldn't imagine what his reaction would be to the knowledge that I was the father of his grandchild...it would make us related by blood.

There was so much I didn't know about

everything, I had been so selfish in turning my back on Jessie that I hadn't even bothered to consider what sort of danger I'd left her in.

What the fuck had I done?

The memory of the first words that came into my head after I'd stabbed Tom was never more relevant. My mind was heading for information overload and I didn't know if I could take any more.

"She moved in with me after your Dad died. She's Mikey's brother after all. I couldn't turn her away."

I felt relieved. Mary was a good woman, so normal even after what she had been through. It couldn't have been easy for her to bring up a child conceived by rape, to be visually reminded every day by such a barbarous act.

"What about Mikey?" I asked, "What does he make of it all?"

"He's quiet, withdrawn, he's got a lot of things on his mind but he won't talk to me. I want to help him but I don't know what to say. Don't get me wrong I appreciate you getting him away from Dean but couldn't you have done it another way? Finding out who and what his father was should never have happened. He asked me if it was true and I had to go over everything again, he's barely said a word to me since."

Yet again I was reminded just how wrong my actions had been. I hadn't done it to help Mary I had been much more cynical than that. My only intention was to use Mikey for my own ends, as a means to validate my desire to get even with Tom. He was offered to me as a tool, a gift from God, divine intervention to put things right, in my crazed mind he was the sacrificial lamb and I'd led him to the slaughter, the slaughter of Tom. Only I didn't succeed, my justifiable intentions to rid the world of someone as evil as Tom had failed.

I gritted my teeth, I knew I should apologise to Mary for using Mikey as a pawn and for betraying her confidence. She'd told me a secret about her past and I'd let her down but what was the point in saying sorry? What would that change? Not a thing but I said it anyway and I don't think she even realised there was a lack of conviction in my voice, her mind as well as mine was elsewhere.

I didn't want to talk to her any more, I'd learnt enough about Jessie and Mikey to know that there were still problems to overcome, problems that I couldn't do much about.

We looked at each other for ages until Mary broke the silence.

"Nick wants to visit."

"Mulvey?" I said in shock, "what the hell does

he want?"
I still harboured a fair amount of anger over the
way Mulvey had turned me in. I'd told him I'd
wanted time to sort a few things out and having
the opportunity to talk to Mary was one of them. I
wasn't sure I wanted to see him again.

"I've been seeing him for a couple of months."
I looked at her in disbelief; Mary and Mulvey
together just didn't seem to add up. She wasn't
unattractive but she was far from Mulvey's type.
His personality demanded a lot from a partner
and Mary wasn't vivacious enough. Maybe it was a
rebound romance because of what happened with
Sami but I doubted it. Mulvey was up to
something and it left me no choice, I had to see
him.

The bell sounded to let us know that visiting was
over and in a way I was glad because it meant I
didn't have to pursue any details of her
relationship with Mulvey, anything I wanted to
know was best heard from the man himself. We
said goodbye and I wished her good luck in
sorting things out with Mikey.

"Time heals everything." I said, although from
my experience that had never been a truthful
statement to make.

CHAPTER TWENTY-NINE

I'd spent an hour with Mary and she'd left me with a lot of information that I hadn't expected to have to think about. Her unscheduled arrival meant that I realised more than ever a lot of my past had to be dealt with. I had finally begun to believe what the counsellors had been telling me...that it would make it easier if I was to talk to my friends outside prison.

Although Mary was angry with me because of what I'd done to her 'mother and son' relationship I felt that we could help each other by talking about it. The only doubt I had was her involvement with Mulvey and what his true intentions were. I tried to imagine just what was going through his mind. I knew he hadn't been able to understand what I'd done in his club and as I hadn't been able to explain why I guessed he had turned himself into some sort of private detective to glean together as much information as he possibly could. I wondered if he had any idea of how large a can of worms he was going to open up and how ultimately it would lead him to discover how many things were interconnected.

How was he going to react when he found out about Tom and Sami's relationship?

I tried to put it out of my mind, I still had a fortnight or longer before I set eyes on him so worrying about what he was up to could wait.

An image of Jessie appeared in my head, she was lying on a hospital bed legs wide apart screaming out my name. She looked in absolute agony but I still managed a smile. I heard the midwife calmly telling her to push but that just seemed to make Jessie yell even more. I could make out the baby's head stained with blood and then that was it, the image disappeared. No baby, no Jessie...nothing.

I wished I was there with her. I wanted to know that everything was o.k. I wanted to know what it was...did I have a daughter or a son?

The day dragged and I was really on edge, every second was spent waiting for the news that I was a father. Being confined to my cell put an added pressure on me and I nervously paced up and down what little floor space we had. My new cellmates were just as eager for the birth to be announced as I was genuinely pissing them off with my non-stop sighing and questioning of the ignorance of the prison authorities.

"What are they doing?" I kept repeating, "She must have had it by now. Why won't they let me know?"

Lights out came and there was still no news. I lay on my bunk fully dressed, tossing and turning. I don't know what I expected because it wasn't as though I was going to be allowed to see it, why couldn't I just relax and wait for the inevitable outcome.

Morning came and I still hadn't been informed but deep down I knew I wouldn't be disturbed during the night, not that it had any affect on my sleep...I didn't get any. Finally at ten twenty five I had a message to go to the governor's office. I was elated, beaming broadly as I was escorted down the corridor only to have my world come crashing down once more.

The image from the previous day came flooding back into my mind. Jessie in hospital, pushing, the baby's head appearing and then the blackness...no Jessie, no baby. Had someone been trying to tell me something then? The blackness cleared and the vision sprang back into life, Jessie still pushing frantically trying to get the baby out of her body, its tiny head smeared with blood, its skin a deathly shade of white, the cord around its neck...the cord...around its neck.

"Stop Jessie...STOP!" I shouted at her, "Stop pushing!"

I banged my fists into the governor's table as I shouted, hearing his words of sorrow. Sorry?

What the fuck was he sorry about? What the fuck did he care? I'd just lost the one thing that was going to be the start of me getting my life in order...the word sorry was not going to help in the slightest.

CHAPTER THIRTY

I was driven out of prison that afternoon in an ambulance, taken to a secure mental institution heavily sedated. I had no recollection of anything I had done in the aftermath of having been told that my child had died in what was supposed to be the beautiful experience of being born. Maybe I had attacked the governor, maybe I had tried once again to harm myself, I had no idea but whatever it was it resulted in me being held in a psychiatric hospital. Did they think I was mentally insane and that it was necessary for me to be dealt with in such a way?

They were wrong.

Apart from the first few hours of which I could remember nothing I was totally in control of my mind and what was going on around me. It was like I was in a drug enhanced trance once again only I hadn't been as calm or felt as serene ever before. Maybe they were feeding me some sort of drug that had in effect turned me into a vegetable but I didn't think it was possible, surely that would have destroyed my thought process.

I was aware that I was strapped to my bed and

there was a drip attached to my right arm. Was that for food or a steady supply of sedative in their attempts to have complete control over me?

Time became meaningless, I hadn't any idea whether it was night or day, everything just merged into emptiness. I spent all my time either staring into space or drifting off to sleep. Countless doctors and psychiatrists appeared clutching clipboards and taking notes gently trying to cajole me into talking but although I was totally aware that they were there and what they were saying I didn't speak or acknowledge their existence. Occasionally I wanted to say something, to get things off my chest but stopped myself from doing so. I wanted to distance myself from everything and everybody and it became like I was playing a game that only the strongest mind would win. I was sure that they would give up first, disregard me as severely mentally disturbed, someone who would never respond to treatment.

Jessie visited all the time; at least she always seemed to be there whenever I woke up. She talked non-stop and even though I could hear every word I just stared blankly through her. She kept on and on about how sorry she was for losing the baby, that yet again everything was her fault. I knew she was searching for my forgiveness but I didn't think that forgiveness was mine to give.

FADING LIGHT

I thought back to the vision I'd had of her pushing and hearing my voice telling her to stop. Something was formulating deep inside my mind, I kept thinking that someone was trying to tell me something, something about that vision. What did it mean? Did I have some sort of gift? It wasn't the first time I'd seen 'events'...imagining things that weren't really there.

I was being irrational; all my visions were obviously related to my experiences with drugs. My body was used to images being portrayed on my mind thanks to heroin so how was I to know that the mental effects of that drug didn't stay in my memory for a long time, maybe my mind had been poisoned so badly that I couldn't differentiate between fact and fiction. I thought back again to when I was so dependent on getting heroin that I had forgotten who I was but that didn't hold true any more because I knew who I was, I had never been more sure about myself and although I was no longer talking to anyone I had an inner determination to deal with all the shit that still existed. Others could make their own judgements about me but whatever they decided they would be wrong.

The days passed and the deliberate vegetative state that I'd imposed on myself seemed to be feeding me a new strength, I hadn't given any hint of possible violent outbursts so I was no longer strapped to my bed. Jessie wheeled me around the hospital in a wheelchair mainly down to the day room to mix with the other patients in an attempt to get me to interact and hopefully to get me to talk but I just found the whole escapade amusing and on occasions it was difficult not to laugh out loud. I was trying as hard as I could to be oblivious to everything going on around me yet I was sitting in a room full of lunatics who for whatever reason didn't know who they were or what they were doing, it was nearly enough to drive me insane.

The more I had to put up with the harder it became for me not to say anything just to be able to get out of there, but I couldn't, I had to use the time to devise a plan. I was out of prison and I had to use the opportunity to my benefit. I didn't want to go back to jail and its filthy conditions because I knew it would once again send me to the depth of despair but I didn't want to act like a vegetable for too much longer.

I felt safe where I was, maybe it was having Jessie around all the time, even though I wasn't talking to her I felt as though she was helping me, giving me the therapy I needed but to make any further progress I needed to talk; I just didn't know how to.

In the end my mind was made up for me in a way I wasn't expecting and it triggered a whole new range of emotions I hadn't experienced before and never thought I would.

Jubilation.

It wasn't something that had ever crossed my mind but why I saw it as a reason to celebrate albeit on the inside was easy to explain. Dad's suicide had been avenged...Dean was dead.

It was the first time I had physically responded to Jessie's voice. It had come as such a shock when she told me that I couldn't stop the natural reaction of turning my face towards hers, my eyes sparkling, inquisitive, eager to know more. Jessie noticed my interest and I knew it was finally time to talk.

"Take me outside." I whispered.

The hospital was set in its own grounds and I had been wheeled around many times before. Therapeutic it was meant to be and in lots of ways it was, it showed me quite convincingly that what I desperately wanted was my freedom, to have back what most people took for granted, to be part of the real world again.

My first question was a little odd but something that had been gnawing away inside my head since I'd been detained in hospital.

"What was it?"

"What?"

Jessie was baffled by my words.

"The baby...what was it?"

In all the time Jessie had been visiting and talking about it she had only referred to our child as the baby.

"A boy, why?"

"I needed to know, it just makes it real somehow."

"Does it make it any easier knowing what it was? Boy or girl, it was our child and I killed it."

Jessie was still beating herself up about how our son died and although I accepted it wasn't her fault I still had subconscious thoughts...what if she hadn't pushed, had held back and let the doctors unravel the cord from around his neck, would he still be alive? Was he dead before his head appeared? These were questions that needed to be addressed at some point, I needed to talk to Jessie about it to help her through her own personal crisis but it wasn't the right time, I had something more important on my mind. I had to console her though just in case she lapsed into another sorrowful outburst, I'd heard everything about how she felt so many times I knew it off by heart...I had to change the subject.

"How did he die?"

"The cord was around his neck..."

"No, not our son," I quickly interrupted, "Dean."

Jessie was silent for a moment, I'm sure she was disappointed that I no longer wanted to talk about our son but surely she knew that Dean's death was, at least to me, more relevant. I knew I was being selfish, self centred in once again putting my own feelings first but Dean was the bastard who had ultimately made Dad kill himself and I wanted to know if he had suffered in his own death.

"He was found face down in a river about three miles out of town." Jessie said with what could only be described as an air of contempt; she couldn't disguise the fact that she had bad feelings towards Dean even though he was her brother.

In a way I could understand that she had problems with him, he obviously knew I had got her pregnant and as I was the cause of all the crap in his life I guessed he would have been particularly nasty to Jessie. I suddenly felt I was no better than Tom in many respects; I hadn't been as destructive towards others as he had but I had still managed to influence the actions of other people.

"How did it happen?"

I needed to know whether it was an accident or something a little more sinister.

"The police don't think it was an accident."

"Murder?"

"It was close to one of 'their' meeting places, you knew he was gay didn't you? They think it was a lover's tiff that got out of hand. Anything's possible with Dean, I'm just surprised that it wasn't him doing the killing."

I was right, there was real bitterness seeping out of Jessie and it got worse.

"I'm fucking glad...he wanted to kill you and he even tried to punch me in the stomach while I was pregnant..."

I felt a sense of anger; he had tried to kill my baby? That was going too far even for someone like Dean, I was glad he was dead.

"...Mikey stopped him, threatened him and for some reason Dean backed down. It was as though Dean still had feelings for Mikey, feelings that he seemed to find difficult to control."

I felt slightly sick at what Jessie was intimating, Dean still cared about Mikey in the way he used to before he found out they were brothers? I knew it was natural to care about previous partners but in this case? Surely that couldn't be true, not that it mattered, it was irrelevant and I didn't want to think about it. Dean was dead and I had cause to celebrate.

Jessie was quiet for ages after that, she seemed

content to just push me around the hospital grounds and although I had plenty I wanted to say I left her alone with her thoughts.

"Nick still wants to see you." She said eventually.

I'd forgotten.

Mary had told me the day before my son had died and that event had overshadowed a lot of things that were on my mind.

Mulvey.

What did he want? It must have been important for him to keep on asking to see me and that convinced me even more that he was up to something. I was sure that Jessie would go home and tell everyone that I was talking again and I didn't want her to do that, I still needed time to sort myself out mentally without interference from anyone.

We'd been outside for over an hour and as there weren't many other patients around I was pretty certain that no one had noticed I was holding a conversation with Jessie. It was important to me that the doctors didn't find out, I didn't want them fussing around thinking they had made a breakthrough, that I was on the road to recovery, a recovery that to me would lead straight back to the hell of prison.

"Jessie," I whispered, "please don't tell anyone

I'm talking to you."

"Why? It's good news, it's a positive sign."

"Please," I whispered a little louder, "I don't want to go back to jail. I'm better off here, can't you see that?"

Jessie told me that she hadn't seen it like that, for some reason she just thought I was in hospital and the moment I was better I would be allowed home...home with her. She had almost become as detached from reality as I had.

"Tell Nick to come visit, tell him you think I'm responding to treatment, tell him you think I can understand what you are saying to me. Just don't tell him the truth, I'll do that when he gets here."

She was reluctant; she thought that the longer I stayed silent the more likely it was that I would be locked up forever. I had to be cruel again, telling her that if she didn't do as I asked then I definitely would go back to being silent.

"You wouldn't dare, they'll never let you out of here."

"I'm NOT going back to jail...I'll do whatever it takes."

Jessie left almost immediately and I was a little perturbed at the way she did it. I had hoped to carry on talking to her about Dean and more than that I wanted to know about Tom. I needed to know how he had been treating her, had she even seen him? Did he know I was the father of her child? Did he even know if I actually knew her?

I wanted to know all about Dean's relationship with his father, how it had affected him, I'd heard some things from Mary but that was more to do with Mikey and Dean rather than Tom. I'd been sensible enough not to mention Tom more than I had to because of what he'd done to Mary and as I'd caused such a rift between her and Mikey I hadn't wanted to run the risk of alienating her any further.

Jessie had pushed my wheelchair back into the main building and I had to return to my original vegetative state, I began to feel frustrated and for a moment considered giving up on my pretence. Was it really worth it? What was the actual point? Something in my head told me to stick with it like I was being led to a final date with destiny, finding my own personal holy grail.

Dean was dead and Tom soon would be.

Someone was putting words into my mind! Tom soon would be? Why had I suddenly thought that? Maybe I was just connecting everything together in the way I wanted it concluded. The final piece in the jigsaw needed to be put in place and until it was then nobody could ever move forward, least of all myself. I suddenly felt jealous of whoever had killed Dean and I didn't know why.

CHAPTER THIRTY-ONE

It was another three days before I saw Jessie again and I tortured myself with so many different thoughts about her prolonged absence. She'd been to see me virtually every day since I'd been admitted but it seemed that the very moment I'd started talking she'd disappeared, abandoned me to whatever fate I had coming.

I couldn't talk to anyone such was my determination not to be 'discovered' and returned to jail so apart from mealtimes I was just ignored, left in the day room for hours on end with only a bunch of lunatics for company.

I tried to form all the events of the past into some sort of coherent story but it always had one episode that didn't make any sense.

Who killed Dean and why?

I hadn't known Dean and Mikey at all and they had only come into my life as a means to get at Tom, their gay relationship being a perfect scenario for the way my fucked up mind had been working at the time.

Jessie had said that Dean was killed near a known gay haunt and that the police had said the likelihood of his death was a lover's tiff. I couldn't believe that it was true. How old was Dean? Sixteen? Seventeen? I didn't think that he was old enough or sexually active enough to be playing that sort of scene, there was no way I could believe that he was seeing anyone other than Mikey and the chances of him finding someone else so soon after discovering Mikey was his brother didn't add up. He was too preoccupied with causing trouble for Dad and Jessie than to be out looking for love, too busy looking for revenge for what I'd done to Tom.

Tom.

Something clicked.

Tom's last sight as I stabbed him...Dean naked...Mikey with his penis in his mouth...it was meant to have been and I could that see it was...Tom's worst nightmare!

It had to be, I had to be right, everything was pointing towards that fact...Tom had murdered Dean.

I could feel beads of sweat trickling down my forehead as I sat in my wheelchair. The thought that I had solved the mystery of who had killed Dean had exhausted and exhilarated me. I desperately needed to be away from the day room and I desperately needed to speak to Jessie.

Getting back to my room was quite easy and it

was something I'd done before, I deliberately wet myself. For much of my time in hospital I only wore pyjamas and it was a simple task to arrange my body so that a stream of urine would splash out onto the tiled floor soaking my clothing in the process. I felt it added a touch of reality to the game I was playing, if I wasn't in control of my mind then I couldn't be expected to be in control of my bodily functions.

I immediately attracted the attention of a couple of nurses who tended to my misdemeanour, leading me back to my room to clean me up. Thankfully they left me there when they had finished and I was grateful that I'd achieved my objective.

My conclusion that Tom had murdered Dean was still fresh in my mind and I was becoming more and more convinced that it was an actual fact. It didn't matter to me that I had no positive proof but the feeling was so strong because of what I'd put him through that it wouldn't have been possible for anyone else to want him dead. In my mind Tom was such a violent person that that was the only way he could deal with what to him must have been so devastating and hard to accept. Jessie had to be told, I had to tell her what I'd worked out, that Tom had killed another member of her family, but then I suddenly realised I couldn't, it would mean telling her the truth, the truth about everything. I couldn't remember what I'd told her in the past, how I'd explained why I'd stabbed Tom in the first place. I hadn't told her that I'd lured Dean and Mikey to set a trap for Tom, how would she feel once I'd confessed to that? I'd told so many lies to her to conceal my own past would she ever believe anything I told her in the future?

Shit.

I'd made such a mess of everything that getting out of it had become seemingly impossible. I had no choice I had to keep it to myself there was still so much I didn't know. Once again I'd let my imagination run riot and made assumptions based on my own feelings whether it was true or not hadn't mattered.

I didn't dwell on it much longer because Jessie finally turned up to see me, the opportunity to talk to her about whether Tom had killed Dean or not didn't arise because she'd brought Mulvey with her. I adopted my vegetative pose when I heard his booming voice outside my door until I felt comfortable enough to believe that Jessie hadn't told him anything. The first ten minutes was a bit of a charade, Mulvey was his usual genial, jovial self telling me all about himself and his friendship with Mary as I just sat there slumped in my chair deliberately docile. Jessie did her bit, prompting Mulvey on the rare occasions he was lost for words.

"Just talk about anything," she said, "the doctors think that a friendly voice from the past could act as a trigger."

Eventually I looked around and asked Jessie to leave the room, sort out a few cups of tea so, that I could talk to Mulvey in private. He was somewhat shocked.

"What's going on?" he demanded.

I waited until Jessie had left the room before answering.

"I'll tell you what I told Jessie," I said, "I'm doing this to keep out of jail, you mustn't tell anyone. I might get rumbled one day but until then..."

I trailed off my sentence looking into Mulvey's eyes. I wanted to judge him by his reaction; I wanted to feel I could trust him to keep his mouth shut. His determination to visit bothered me and as much as I wanted to it was something I couldn't ignore. I had to find out what he was up to.

"It's great to see you!" the big man beamed thrusting his right hand towards me. At once I felt intimidated and tentatively responded to his greeting by loosely shaking his hand.

He didn't give me a chance to speak.

"I'm sorry to hear about your troubles, it can't be easy for you."

Easy? I was sure Mulvey didn't mean to say it as flippantly as he did but easy? What the fuck did he know? Had he ever had to deal with the hell that had been my life? I felt our conversation was going to deteriorate into an argument and I wanted to tell him to fuck off there and then but I couldn't, I had to let him continue. If he said anything that was upsetting to me then I had to take it on the chin, deal with it on my own after he had gone.

"What do you want?" I asked as calmly as I could.

"The truth."

That was it, the one word that struck more fear into me than any other. It was something that I'd never had the courage to face up to and yet I knew that it was the only way I could ever come close to putting the past behind me, that and death but I'd done the suicide thing before, more than once, and I knew I wasn't going to go down that road again. Maybe it was finally time to come clean about one or two things, maybe it was time to be a little more honest.

I tried to think back to what I'd told Mulvey, whether I'd lied to him like I had Jessie but I remembered I hadn't told him anything. I tried to imagine what it was he wanted to know but couldn't, it was up to him to ask me questions.

"I'm sorry I turned you in but I didn't think I had any choice."

"I thought you were a friend, I needed time, I needed to talk to people...explain."

"Who to? Jessie? Your Dad? Or..." Mulvey hesitated "...or Mary?"

I began to feel I was right about Mulvey, he was definitely up to something and he was using Mary, why else would he mention her in such a way? I asked him straight.

"Why are you seeing Mary?"

"Because I feel something for her."

"You're lying!"

Mulvey didn't have chance to reply as Jessie reappeared with the tea. She took one look at the two of us staring at each other before asking me if everything was all right.

"Can you leave us alone for a while."

It was an order not a question and although Jessie was reluctant she did as she was told.

"You said you wanted the truth but you have to be honest with me as well."

I was offering Mulvey a compromise, my honesty in return for his, I felt that if I could convince him I was being truthful then I could get out of him what he was up to. Mulvey had always been open with me in the past and it wasn't always easy for him to keep a secret, it was a characteristic of his that would make any questions I asked him answered sincerely.

Up until that point Mulvey had been standing and apart from my wheelchair I had the only seat in the room. I couldn't give it up in case any of the doctors or nursing staff happened to come in and I had to play dumb again. I watched Mulvey intently as I waited for his reply and I could see him physically change before my very eyes. He sighed a deep sorrowful sigh as if a burden had been lifted from his shoulders and he slumped his huge frame down onto my bed.

"O.k," he mumbled, "you're right. I was just trying to work things out in my head."

"By using Mary?"

"In a way...yes."

"I think you had better explain."

"It was a shock you know, finding out what you'd done. You were supposed to be looking after my club while I was trying to come to terms with Sami's death."

Sami.

I hadn't forgotten about her, she was a part of everything as well. A far bigger part now that Mulvey was getting himself involved. I had to be careful what I said to him, maybe I couldn't be as truthful as I'd promised at least for Jessie's sake after all it was her father that Sami had left Mulvey for. Shit, this was getting too complicated. Why did Mulvey have to get involved with Mary? Why couldn't he just disappear from the scene altogether. Everything would be so much easier if he wasn't around. I had to face facts though, he WAS around and things were, if I wasn't careful, going to get out of control. I listened to Mulvey; I was going to say as little as I thought I could get away with.

"It made things worse, I came back to bury myself in my business but you destroyed that. I almost lost the club as well as Sami. I couldn't open again for three weeks, I lost a fortune. People kept away, I had nothing to do. Everything was getting on top of me and the only person who could help me was you."

"But you turned me in!"

"I know and I said I'm sorry, I really thought I was doing it for the best. You seemed so screwed up I was worried for you. I was going to help, get a solicitor, you would have only got six months for G.B.H. but they let you out and you went and did it again...tried to kill him. It played on my mind so much I had to find out why."

"What for? Why should it concern you?"

"You were my friend, you helped me when Sami died. I felt I owed you something."

Mulvey knew more than he was letting on, I was sure of that but he was taking too long to tell me exactly what. I didn't want to know all the little details of how he felt, I just wanted to know what he knew.

"What exactly have you found out?"

"Nothing for definite, I know it involves Mary."

Mulvey was still being too vague, it was time to try a different tactic, I had to start questioning him.

"How did you meet Mary?"

"Through Jessie really."

I was a little surprised, why would Jessie introduce Mary to Mulvey?

"I had nothing to do, plenty of time on my hands to try and understand what made you want to kill someone, it seemed so out of character. It was easy at first, names and pictures in papers, Tom and Dean being father and son, I just took it from there. I had to contact Jessie to see how you were, she was cold towards me but I just thought she was blaming me for you being inside, you know...for turning you in. I stayed on the scene mainly talking to your Dad hoping for some snippet of information, anything that would help me understand but then he died. I found out where Jessie had moved to and that's how I met

FADING LIGHT

Mary. We got to know each other as friends, just by talking I found out Jessie and Mikey were related and gradually things started fitting into place, Dean and Mikey being related as well. I had to know more so I made Mary my target, I had to get her into bed in an effort to find out more but so far she hasn't told me anything. I know there's something that connects you and Mary and Tom but I don't know what it is. He is obviously Mikey's dad but that doesn't seem reason enough to want him dead. Where do you fit in? I can't see any reason for murder but I'll find out with or without your help."

I started to feel a little scared, not for myself but for Mary and Jessie. Mulvey was going too far in his quest and for what? He wasn't going to get anything out of it except an extra large dose of unhappiness. He was going to discover that Mary had been raped and worse than that he was going to discover that Tom was Sami's other man.

Shit. To me that meant that Jessie was in danger but what could I do, I had to tell her to get Mulvey away from Mary somehow split them up like I had done with Dean and Mikey but instead I just fucked up the whole situation yet again.

"So," Mulvey said, "what do you know?"

I couldn't tell him I knew nothing because he would know I was lying, I couldn't deny there was something else about the incident because I'd tried to kill Tom but instead of being calm and just saying I'd done it for Mary I let it slip that he was more involved than he could imagine. I instantly regretted it as Mulvey's mood changed rapidly; he rounded on me with an uncharacteristic venom.

"How do you mean? What's it got to do with me?"

"Leave it Nick, forget about it."

A potentially explosive exchange was inadvertently diffused by Jessie returning and I was more than a little grateful. Raised voices would have done far too much damage for me personally but Jessie's reaction was brilliant, she ushered Mulvey out of the room making out that it was the two of them that were the cause of any noise meaning that my cover wasn't blown. Neither of them came back before they went home and that wasn't good news. I knew their journey home would be fraught especially for Jessie and I prayed that she would get through it o.k. Mulvey wasn't the type to hurt anybody but even so the size of the man compared to Jessie would seem quite frightening. I hoped Jessie wouldn't reveal too much to Mulvey but I wasn't overly confident. She knew what I was trying to keep secret from him about his involvement, she knew about Sami and her dad, the only problem was I may have given her the impression that Mulvey knew as well and that was a cause to panic.

I spent the rest of the day and all night worrying about what was happening and I managed to get myself worked up into a right state. All the good I had brought to myself being away from the depressing conditions of prison, all the memories of the past that I'd successfully blocked out of my mind came flooding back, it got so bad that I almost wished I could get my hands on some heroin, just for one night, just to get through it until I saw Jessie again, knew that she was safe.

The thought of drugs made me realise I was still precariously balanced on the edge, forever teetering from one side to the other and I was beginning to think it would only take a slight push to drive me towards insanity, just one incident could be the deciding factor. I prayed and prayed that it wouldn't be that night, I prayed and prayed that nothing would happen to Jessie.

CHAPTER THIRTY-TWO

Jessie arrived early the next morning, she didn't look too good and her mood wasn't much better.

"You lied to me!"

All my overnight fears had immediately been realised but I tried to allay them by being as ignorant as I possibly could.

"What do you mean?"

"You lied to me!" Jessie repeated, "you told me you stabbed Dad because of Nick, he didn't even know him!"

"I didn't lie to you, I did do it for Nick only he didn't know about it."

"Stop it Roo, I'm not stupid, stop lying to me."

"I'm not lying, I did it for Nick...because of what your dad did to his life."

"Then why does Mary think you did it for her then?"

"What?"

"Why does Mary think you did it for her?"

Jessie repeated herself slowly and emphatically like she had discovered a sordid little secret and I felt empty inside like my whole life had been ripped away. All the things I had been keeping away from everyone were beginning to appear out in the open, everyone was beginning to know too much.

Jessie hadn't finished.

"Three different stories Roo, which one do I believe? Are any of them true or is there something else I should know? Did you do it for my mum, Nick or Mary?"

Jessie had every right to be angry just as she had every right to know the truth but if I was going to tell her the truth then it had to be the whole truth and that included my real reason for getting even with Tom. I couldn't reveal my most sensitive secret there and then so I had to play for time, I had to find out exactly what she knew, what it was that Mary and Mulvey had told her. I had to get her to calm down.

"What happened last night?" I asked her.

"What didn't happen," she retorted, "everyone arguing, shouting, it was like living at home again. If it wasn't for Mikey then God knows what would have happened."

It was getting worse by the minute; Mikey was there as well. I began to imagine just what had been said, I could almost feel everybody's hatred directed at me. Everyone had their own happy, content little lives until I had appeared on the scene and what had I done? Sent a tidal wave of devastation through everything. I couldn't do what I wanted to do, sit down in a room with everybody and sort things out peacefully and amicably there was too much bad feeling floating around for that to happen. So what could I do? Sit there and wait until everyone's anger had blown over? There wasn't much chance of that, things were starting to get out of control again even Dean's death was playing a part. I was still convinced that Tom had killed him and I thought about telling Jessie of my theory but judging by her mood she was hardly likely to believe me and I decided it was best to keep my mouth firmly shut.

It was just as well I did as Jessie started talking again only a lot calmer than before.

"I'm sorry Roo, I need to know the truth but I think there's some things you should know first. Last night seemed to be a time for confessions and I learnt a lot, too much really. That's why I'm a little angry...everyone knows more than I do. Maybe I didn't get involved enough at the beginning but I believed what you told me...you stabbed Dad...you got caught...you got jailed...end of story. I wasn't interested in details, I had lost you and I wanted you back, a predictable over emotional teenage girl."

She gave a little nervous laugh and I became all too aware of how young she was.

"I never connected anything together in the way Nick has, I hadn't needed to. O.K. so I know about Dean and Mikey and you told me about Sami and Dad but to me they were just separate issues...until last night."

Jessie bowed her head, her sadness giving her an extra vulnerability and I wanted to reach out and hold her in my arms. I spoke to her softly.

"What happened?"

"Nick got angry in the car on the way home, he wanted to know what you meant about him being involved. I thought he knew, you told me you did it for him, but he hadn't any idea about Sami seeing Dad. He was mad at me, you and especially Dad. Mary got involved when we got home and that's when it got out of hand. She told him you had done it for her to split up Dean and Mikey. I couldn't believe what I was hearing, there was so much shouting until Mikey told Nick that Dad had raped Mary and he was the result. Nick stormed out saying he was going to get Dad and Mikey went after him, I followed and managed to stop Mikey telling him to let Nick do what he wanted to do."

"And?" I interrupted; I wanted to know about Nick and Tom.

"And nothing, I knew he wouldn't find him, he's been working away for the past few months.

He didn't even come back home when Dean was found in the river."

That threw my theory about Dean out of the window. If Tom had been working away then he couldn't possibly have murdered Dean. My thoughts temporarily drifted away from what Jessie was telling me and I was trying to conjure up another suspect who wanted Dean dead but no one in my mind fitted the bill, perhaps the police had been right in their assumption that it had been a sexually related killing.

"I'm sorry." I said to Jessie. I was about to lie to her again and say that I stabbed Tom as a way of revenge for everybody's pain but she spoke first.

"That's not all..." she started, "...there's something else and I don't know how to deal with it."

I didn't know what she meant, she knew everything about everybody's involvement apart from my reason, there was nothing else to know.

"Mikey got himself into a bit of a state and I had to calm him down. He was shaking uncontrollably and I thought it was to do with what had been said about him and his mother, but then he told me something that shook me rigid. He'd still been seeing Dean...for sex."

"But they're brother's!" I almost shouted in my condemnation of what Jessie was telling me.

"I know and I didn't know what to say. He told me they were still having sex while Dad was in a coma in hospital. He said they couldn't give each other up but Dean was getting more and more out of control especially with his hatred towards you. Mikey told me he had a lot of respect for you for what you'd done in stabbing Dad...because of what he'd done to Mary. Like a lot of people, me included, he wished you'd killed him."

I wasn't sure I liked what I was hearing, Mikey was making me out to be some sort of hero, a vigilante sorting out the good from the bad. It wasn't right, I was nothing like that, I was just someone who had become completely fucked up by circumstance. I couldn't understand why he was still seeing Dean for sex but even so I guessed he would have been totally fucked up by his death.

"So how is he coping..." I shuddered as I asked, "...without Dean?"

"That's the problem I can't deal with...Mikey killed him."

That was a bolt right out of the blue, I hadn't even considered Mikey as a possible suspect and if Jessie hadn't told me herself I wasn't sure if I ever would have believed it.

Jessie saw the shocked expression on my face.

"He confessed last night, he said he couldn't stand the guilt, he had to tell someone. He loved

Dean but couldn't stand the pain he was causing other people, you, me, your dad, the thought of Mary finding out he was still having sex with Dean. He wanted Dean to leave us alone but he refused, he said he tried to end their relationship but Dean told him he would kill him first, they had a fight...he said it was self defence..."

"What's he going to do now?"

Jessie shrugged.

"He says he's going to give himself up after the funeral."

"When is that?"

"Friday, the day after tomorrow."

I sat still for a moment, quiet as a mouse as my mind seemed to take on a will of its own, a few thoughts dancing around in my brain.

"Take me outside," I finally said, "I need some fresh air."

CHAPTER THIRTY-THREE

I'd asked Jessie for her address before she left saying that I wanted to start writing to her. I had taken a massive gamble on the state of her mind not being as alert as it should have been considering what she'd been through over the previous twenty four hours. Normally she would have realised that being a supposed 'vegetable' I wouldn't be able to write but I struck lucky and she gave it to me without a second thought. I had no intentions of writing to her, my plan was much more devious than that, I was going to try and escape.

Asking her to take me outside was not for the sake of fresh air but to see how the land lied, to case the joint, not as a means to break in but rather to break out. I was fortunate that I had been classed as mentally insane and not criminally insane and the hospital I'd been placed in didn't have the same sort of security as if I'd been certified highly dangerous. Most of my fellow detainees could hardly move they were so disturbed and it was by watching them that I had developed my own afflictions. I was, for the most part, confined to a wheelchair and as I'd been there for a while hardly anybody took any notice of me. I'd made sure Jessie had taken me around the grounds a few times so that I could be sure my escape route wouldn't be too difficult in the dark.

I knew I was running the risk of adding time to my sentence but I didn't really care, that was something to worry about in the future, what was on my mind at that moment was the overriding necessity to escape.

It was two thirty in the morning and I was freezing cold, I'd left the window in my room open since early in the evening; one less noise to make when the time came. Because of the nature of the hospital I was in there was only a skeleton staff employed at night and although I had no idea of the level of security outside I didn't think it would be that heavy.

It turned out to be easier than I'd imagined. With adrenalin pumping ferociously around my body I felt like an out of control steam engine its pistons hammering up and down in their desperation to go faster and faster. I sprinted across the lawn to the perimeter wall where I briefly waited, checking that I hadn't been seen. I couldn't wait too long, speed was of an essence and I headed swiftly towards an area where all the dustbins were stored. They were housed under a small lean-to and I'd thought earlier that it wouldn't be too difficult to use a couple of bins to stand on in order to reach the roof.

It worked perfectly and even though I made a bit of noise dragging the bins into position I was up on the roof in less than a minute. I peered over the edge down onto the street below. My beating heart slowed as I faced up to my next obstacle...a twelve foot drop.

I couldn't just leap off, it was too high and that would have run the risk of me injuring myself. I stepped off the roof onto the top of the wall and gingerly lowered myself down a couple of inches at a time until I was hanging full stretch by my fingertips. It had become a situation I couldn't turn back from and I had to let go, a six foot drop into the dark not knowing what would happen when my feet made contact with the ground. I prayed that the impact wouldn't be too severe.

I let go, grazing the side of my face as I slid down. I felt as though I could somehow slow my progress by grasping at the wall but it made no difference...I still hit the pavement with force. My ankles gave way under the pressure and I felt a sharp pain shoot up my legs forcing me to crumple like a deck of cards into a heap on the ground. Even though the initial pain was making me draw breath sharply I couldn't afford to lie there until it subsided. I had no choice but to grin and bear it, I had to get away as fast as possible.

I pulled myself to my feet and limped off down the road, I had no idea where I was going and I didn't even know if it was in the right direction, I just had to keep moving. I hobbled aimlessly for about thirty minutes, ducking into shop doorways every time I heard a vehicle approach and my mind flashed back to the time when I was fleeing the scene of my crime, a desperate criminal with the rest of the world in hot pursuit. Thankfully though the pain caused by my jump off the wall had begun to abate and I was grateful that there seemed to be no lasting damage. It was time to stop and take stock, assess the situation and plan my next move.

I had to work out how far I was from where Jessie lived and how long it was going to take to get there. I knew it couldn't be too far because Jessie visited most days, thirty miles at the most but that was still far enough without any transport. I checked my watch, it was ten past three.

Looking up the road away from the hospital I saw I was almost at a roundabout and I hurried towards it hopeful that the signposts would give me a clue to my whereabouts.

I had mixed feelings when I got there. I was fortunate that I was headed in the right direction but I had a lot further to travel than I'd thought. Forty-eight miles. I couldn't believe I was so far away and almost wanted to give up but then a persuasive thought struck me...Jessie...she had been travelling that distance most days just to see me slumped in a wheelchair, that was impressive, that was dedication. If she could do it so many times then what sort of person would I be if I couldn't do it once. I had to do it anyway, I was being told to. Too much had happened with Jessie, Mulvey, Mikey and Mary. I knew something horrific was going to happen and I had to be there. In my mind Mulvey and Mikey were unstable, likely to do absolutely anything and they both had one probable target...Tom.

I thought back to a vision I'd had after I'd heard about Dean...Tom would be next.

It was all becoming clear.

Tom was going to die but I wasn't going to let Mulvey or Mikey do it. It was my right...it had to be me.

CHAPTER THIRTY-FOUR

It took over four hours to reach my home town, my desperation led me to hitch part of the way, but it had given me time to think. I knew I had reached a point where everything had to be sorted out once and for all, to bring everything to a conclusion with no loose ends and if that meant that I had to kill Tom to achieve it then that was what I was going to do. From what Jessie had told me I knew that Mulvey was going to confront Tom at some point and if he was as intelligent as he was making himself out to be then he would already have predicted that Tom would definitely be at Dean's funeral. No matter what he thought about Dean's choice of lifestyle he was still his only son and he had to pay his last respects.

Mikey on the other hand was unpredictable, I couldn't rationally contemplate what he was going to do, he had become in my mind a bit of a loose cannon. For someone who had seemed so timid he had already killed once even though Jessie had said he'd done it in self-defence I wasn't so sure. His admittance to her that he was going to give himself up after Dean's funeral had set me thinking that he was planning something.

What else had she told me?

That he had some sort of respect for me in trying to murder Tom in revenge for Mary's rape, that was quite a disturbing thought. He was the by product of that rape and his hatred of Tom would be pretty equal to mine and I had as much cause as any one to want Tom's life to end. I was convinced that Mikey intended to murder Tom as well.

I'd felt jealous when Jessie told me of Dean's death, jealous of whoever had killed him and I was getting jealous again. It was up to me to sort things out. Mikey had already murdered someone, Tom had tasted blood too...he'd murdered my beautiful Alice and her suffering had still to be avenged. If Tom was going to die then it had to be by my hands.

I still had things to sort out though, if I was going to kill Tom then I had to see Jessie, I had to have her help to be able to make it to the funeral. I had no intention of telling her what I really wanted to do so I had to lie; I had to make her see that I was only there to stop Mikey and Mulvey from making a mistake. I also had something else to tell her, something far more important, something I should have been honest about a long time before. If I was sorting things out with no loose ends then

I had to lay my own ghosts to rest, I had to tell her everything about my life.

She was easy to find, even though I'd made sure that she had given me her address I'd already worked out that she travelled to see me in hospital by train and that's where I went first...the train station. I checked the departure times on the timetable and then sat myself down on a bench to wait. It was nearly two hours before she turned up and I was cold and starving. I spotted her walking across the car park outside the station and rushed to meet her. She was mortified that I was there.

"What the hell are you doing?" she cried, "They'll put you away for life!"

"I had to see you, I had to warn you." I replied before telling her of my fears about Mulvey and Mikey.

She tried to make out that she didn't care, that she wasn't going to the funeral anyway and that Mulvey could do what the fuck he liked.

"But what about Mikey?" I said, "don't you care about what happens to him?"

Finally I'd hit a nerve, I knew she'd grown close to Mikey over the months I'd been locked away, he'd protected her from many things and was acting like a real brother to her. I told her he needed her help, that if it was true and he had killed Dean in self defence then it was important that he didn't kill again. A jury might accept a self defence plea in one case but if he was up on two counts of murder then there was no way he was ever going to be believed.

"Can we go for a walk?" I suggested, "I've got a lot of things I want to say to you."

Jessie didn't say a word but she followed me willingly as I took her hand in mine and made off towards a local park. I led her across the vast lawns and sat down on a bench next to the pond. It was wonderful to feel the freshness of the open air and the freedom to once again walk with Jessie made what I wanted to tell her that little bit easier.

"You wanted me to be truthful and honest with you," I said as I looked into her eyes, "so I'm going to tell you everything no matter how painful it is."

"You don't have to." Jessie said, but deep down I knew she wanted to know.

"If I get upset or start crying then don't stop me...I have to bare my soul completely and totally, it's the only way I can do this."

I almost started crying straight away such was the thought of the emotion that I was about to reveal.

"I hate your dad, Tom, so much it's almost impossible to describe. I grew up with him here in this town, we went to school together and hung around together afterwards because there were only half a dozen at most who were the same age as me on our estate. It was either that or rot in my bedroom on my own. He bullied me, him and his mates, for as long as I could remember but it didn't matter...I got used to it, it was their way of having fun. It didn't get too far out of hand because of Alice, your mum, she always made him stop when she thought he was going too far until..."

I stopped for a moment as a lump started to form in my throat. Jessie gripped my hand and squeezed it tight, I thought of Alice and a single tear dripped from my eye.

"...I'm sorry, this is the worst bit...it was my sixteenth birthday and I was out with them all, we were drinking and joking around getting a little pissed until I was sort of kidnapped. They blindfolded me and took me to a farm just outside of town. That's where it happened, my own personal hell on earth, that's where I...I..."

I was really crying, letting go of everything that I'd been harbouring inside for far too long. I couldn't believe that I was actually going to tell someone, it was like admitting to myself that it had really happened.

"You don't have to tell me," Jessie said, "if it's that bad then I don't have to know."

"I've got to," I replied wiping the tears forcibly

away from my eyes, "I've got to get it out."
I sat still for a moment looking around the park, watching the ducks and swans gliding across the water. Everything was so relaxed and peaceful, the exact opposite of how I was feeling.

"I was raped!"
I'd finally said it and I couldn't speak any more, the tears were flowing like a torrent soaking everything in their path. The relief I'd expected to feel on saying those few words didn't happen instead I felt an incredible surge of anger and the image of Tom hysterically laughing flashed across my mind. If he had been there at that moment I would have killed him with my bare hands.

"We need to get away from here."
Jessie whispered into my ear, she had her arms around my neck and was kissing me intensely on every part of my face that she could. It was her way of showing me how she felt, that everything was going to be o.k. but it wasn't what I wanted, I had so much more to tell her.
I pushed her away.

"Please don't," I sobbed, "I have to tell you everything."
Jessie must have felt hurt but she didn't let it show instead she told me that I was going back with her to Mary's house assuring me that nobody was there and not likely to be until later that

afternoon.

I let her lead me out of the park and off towards our destination. The vision of Tom was with me all the way and I could feel the anger welling fiercely. There was no doubt about it, he only had hours to live.

Jessie ushered me inside as soon as we arrived clipping the door chain into place so that no one could enter without her knowledge. My images of Tom had become interspersed with pictures of all the low points of my life and it was as if I was replaying all the scenes in my mind in an effort to get them right before I passed them on to Jessie. I didn't want to tell her but if I didn't get everything out into the open right then I knew I wouldn't ever get another chance. The time, finally, was right.

"I was in love with Alice."

"You told me that, you also told me that was why you stabbed Tom."

"I know and in a way that's the truth. I told you that she always stopped Tom when things were going too far but this time she didn't. I thought I was making love to her, she was saying things to me while it was happening and then they made me look. It was a nightmare and it's here in my head all the time, not just some of the time but all the fucking time."

"Roo, I'm sorry, I don't know what to say."

"Don't say anything, just listen and understand why I'm the way I am."

I needed a drink and asked Jessie if she had any scotch, it had been a long time since I'd tasted alcohol and it was as good as I'd remembered as she dutifully returned with a glassful.

"Thanks." I said as I emptied the contents down my throat.

I felt a lot calmer afterwards and felt it was going to be easy to relay the full extent of my horror.

"Alice was so full of guilt about everything, couldn't apologise enough. I found out she had been blackmailed into it because of some pictures Tom had taken. I forgave her because I loved her and we started seeing each other until one night Tom raped her. I went crazy, I wanted to kill him then...I begged her to leave him and I really thought she would but then she found out she was pregnant and chose to stay with him. I vowed one day I would get my revenge."

I motioned to my glass and Jessie went off to replenish it, this time bringing the bottle back as well.

"I went off the rails, always drinking, until the day Dean was born. I went to hospital to see if it looked like me but I was just deluding myself. I couldn't take any more and left home only coming back when Mum got ill...that's when I met you."

"So it's my fault then?" Jessie smiled.

I knew she was only trying to inject a bit of humour into the situation but I wasn't in the mood for laughing. I was dragging my skeletons kicking and screaming out of their cupboards so that I could bury them forever.

"Don't be stupid!" I snapped and the smile vanished from Jessie's face swiftly followed by an apology.

"I met Nick and Mary and discovered that they too had had that bastard fuck up their lives especially Mary...he must have raped her on the night Dean was born. How would Alice have felt had she known that? When you told me about him killing Alice that was it, the final straw, I had to put things right, even up the score, not just for me but everyone including you...only I failed."

"You didn't fail Roo, you made people face up to things, even me. I knew Dad wasn't a good man because of what I saw him do to Mum but did I tell anyone about it? No...I didn't because I was scared, at least you were brave enough to carry out what no one else could."

"I ended up in jail...and for what? So Tom could walk around a free man? How do you think I felt? I still carried all the shit around with me, mine, yours, Mary's, Nick's. How the fuck was I meant to cope? He was still free to do what the fuck he liked. I was helpless, look what happened to Dad! It wouldn't have happened if I had killed Tom. I couldn't forget, it was in my head all the time, I took drugs to block the pain...it was hell in there...far worse than you can imagine...I was forced to..."

I gritted my teeth as I spoke, it was something I didn't want anyone to know but I said it anyway.

"...I was raped again...why do you think I tried to kill myself?"

Jessie looked at me in shock, I think she'd finally realised just how low I'd sunk, how devastated I'd become. I grabbed the bottle and started to pour its contents down my throat, I wasn't going to stop until the bottle was empty. Jessie came to hold me as I drank and I spluttered as her arms wrapped around my body.

"I'm so sorry Roo, I didn't know. It's going to be all right now. Whatever's happened we've still got each other."

Jessie's words were lost on me, they were inconsequential, they had no meaning. We had no future together and after I'd killed Tom she would realise that as well. This was going to be my last day with her and despite the fact that I was going to fuck her life up completely by getting myself a life sentence I had to try and make the last few hours special.

I didn't finish the bottle of scotch, I just let it fall from my grasp onto the floor. I placed my hands on either side of Jessie's face and drew her lips up to meet mine. It was a beautiful feeling as we touched, a vibrant electricity spreading through every vein. A split second thought about giving up on my quest to kill Tom was instantly dismissed It was something that I had to do just as I had to make love with Jessie...one last time.

My hands dropped from her face to her clothing and because of the aggressive nature of my mood I wanted to tear every inch of it from her body. It wasn't the way Jessie wanted it and she backed away slightly.

"Not here...upstairs." she said, the dry hoarseness of her voice showing me just how desperate she was as well.

It didn't last long, twelve months of locked up frustration saw to that, we didn't bother with any of the niceties and I barely had time to get my trousers past my ankles before I was inside her. Like an animal I took her but she didn't complain and I could tell by the sweat pouring out of her every pore that it was just as much a relief for her as it was for me.

We collapsed together in sheer exhaustion afterwards, both clinging on to each other not wanting to let go. Different emotions were racing through our minds, Jessie constantly repeating how much she loved me, wanting me to stay yet all I could think of was saying goodbye. I loved her with all my heart but I knew they were our last moments together.

Jessie fell asleep after we'd made love for a second time, it lasted a lot longer and was much more tender than the first hurried, frenzied attempt. I looked at her lying on the bed gently breathing, a flushed satisfied expression on her face and felt pleased that I'd made her relatively content despite the circumstances of my being there.

I wanted to join her in her slumber as I hadn't managed any sleep in over thirty six hours but I couldn't, I had to take advantage of the quiet. I still had something I wanted to do that I couldn't manage if she was still awake and stuck to my side.

I needed a weapon and I had to find one quick, conceal it somewhere before she'd noticed I'd left her room.

She murmured a couple of times as I gently rolled off the bed and pulled my trousers back on but she didn't wake. I didn't bother with my t-shirt because I was only going to be out of the room for a couple of minutes.

I didn't really have much choice over what I was

going to use as a weapon, something blunt would have been my first choice because I wanted to make his death as brutal as possible to make up for the brutality he had shown me but as much as I wanted to use something like a hammer I realised it wouldn't be the easiest thing to conceal let alone the easiest thing to find. It had to be the same as before...a kitchen knife.

I had a few reservations that everything was happening the way it had first time in Mulvey's club. I'd used the knife but hadn't succeeded in my task. I began to feel that I was going to fail again. Too much of everything was too similar to the past; I'd even made love to Jessie the day before I'd first tried to kill Tom.

A voice entered my head telling me what I already knew, my reservations were only nerves, all my visions in the past had come true and this one was going to be no different...Tom would be next...he had to be...I was determined I wouldn't stop until he was dead.

I grabbed a knife from the kitchen drawer, my heart pounding as a shaft of light through the kitchen window caught the steel blade and sent a flash into my eyes, eyes that were already flashing, sparkling at the sea of blood that I could see before me. Tom lying on his back, hands desperately flailing as I stabbed him ten, twenty, thirty times.

Something moved in the outside world, a cat or a bird, I didn't know what it was but it brought me back to reality and I realised I was wasting time standing transfixed by the knife, I stuffed the blade into one of my pockets careful not to inflict any damage on myself and hurried back upstairs to join Jessie.

"Where have you been?" she said, her eyes still closed as she felt the coldness of my skin on hers.

"Toilet." I lied as I once again pulled her close before drifting off into a much needed sleep.

We were wakened a couple of hours later by a rattling and banging on the front door. The chain was still on and Mary had returned from her lunchtime shift.

"What time is it?" Jessie asked looking decidedly startled.

"Just after three thirty."

"Shit...shit...what am I going to do? She can't find you here."

I almost laughed at Jessie's panic, she was harbouring an escaped criminal and it must have been traumatic for her but I told her not to worry, that it would be o.k.

"Just act natural, Mary won't suspect a thing."

She didn't but the situation only served to remind me of the past. Those few days after Alice had been raped and I'd concealed her in my bedroom without Mum and Dad's knowledge. Where Alice and I had grown so close, fallen ever deeper in love only to have it shattered by her pregnancy and the birth of Dean.

Dean, the thought of that little bastard and what he'd done to Dad, I was glad he was dead and I knew I had every right to feel the way I did. Whatever doubts I'd had in my mind a little earlier vanished forever. I was there for the right reasons and there was no way I was going to fail.

FADING LIGHT

CHAPTER THIRTY-FIVE

The burning candle that was my life had been fading for a long time and now it was finally about to go out. The culmination of eighteen years of pain and suffering was heading towards its rightful conclusion.
I'd spent a lot of time on my own in Jessie's room trying to plan what was going to happen the following day but it was difficult predicting just what part the actions of others would play. I guessed Mikey and Mulvey were up to similar things in their own minds equally convinced that they were about to commit murder. I knew I would have to take my opportunity as soon as it arose; I couldn't afford to hold back just in case one of them got in first.
I spoke to Jessie on the fleeting visits she made to see me, it was difficult for her to spend more than a couple of minutes with me because Mary was in a state, neither Mikey or Mulvey had been in contact since the altercations of the previous night and it increased my belief that they were both out for revenge.
Jessie was beginning to believe it too, she begged

me to make sure I stopped Mikey from getting involved and I promised her I would, that that was my intention, that that was why I'd escaped from the hospital.

The alarm expressed by Mary and Jessie about Mikey being missing had given me extra cause to worry, I got the distinct impression that they were going to inform the police that something was going to happen at Dean's funeral and I tried to make Jessie understand that doing so would incriminate Mikey and if he was to be arrested on suspicion before he'd had chance to do anything and found with a weapon in his possession then how would that look. I asked her not to involve the police but to let me sort it out my way.

I slipped out of the house at four in the morning, chances of being spotted or recognised were likely to be slim at that hour. I'd given no thought to the fact that I was on the run and the possibility that extra police patrols would be in the area never crossed my mind. As it was, nothing happened and the whole town seemed deserted. The lull before the storm was how I put it to myself.

I'd made it to the church within forty minutes and pushed open the heavy oak door to get inside. I was lucky that it was one of the few around that still kept its doors open at night.

Memories of Mum and Dad came flooding back

once I was inside and I was tempted to visit the cemetery, it was likely to be the last chance I ever got. I decided against it, there were already going to be enough final goodbyes, Mum and Dad were good points of my life and I wanted to hold on to those memories.

I went up the stairs that led to the bell tower and through the door leading to the balcony that overlooked the church. Peering over the edge out across the pews and towards the altar I had no feelings of guilt over what was about to happen, just an overwhelming feeling that it was the best place it could occur. Retribution in the eyes of God...let him be the final judge.

I still had no idea how things were going to turn out and I briefly hoped that I'd got it wrong about Mikey and Mulvey, I just wanted it to be him and me, one on one, a wild west shoot out, a gentleman's duel but it wasn't going to be like that more a case of Russian roulette for Mikey, Mulvey and me...we all had the proverbial bullet but didn't know who was going to use it.

I tried to get some sleep but the tension was building rapidly, last time I hadn't had time to think everything happened so fast but this time every second was putting fresh thoughts in my mind. Pictures of Alice and Jessie telling me not to do it, then to do it, intermittently changing their minds, pleading no, begging yes, offering me the knife on a golden cushion. It was if I wasn't a hundred per cent sure that I really was doing the right thing. Final seeds of doubt were being sown, I had a choice...go back to prison and serve my sentence, let Mikey or Mulvey do the killing...who the fuck were they to me anyway? In five years or so I would be the free man and I could go and piss on Tom's grave if I wanted to...someone else would be carrying the can, someone else would have destroyed my demons. Jessie and I could stroll off into the sunset with a happy ending...marriage...kids...

Kids?

That should have been happening already, wasn't that why I was about to do what I had to do? Hadn't my mind been turned forever because I'd lost my son? My future dream had been wiped out. I didn't blame Jessie...I blamed myself, in a perfect world I'd be at home changing nappies...Jessie could still have all that, I couldn't, not ever.

I heard the oak door of the church creak as it was opened and then closed, someone had come in and from my position upstairs I had no idea who. Was it Mikey or Mulvey or someone else? Was it Jessie come looking for me having just found out I wasn't lying next to her in bed? Had she been awake and followed me? For the first time in a long while I was scared, scared because up until that moment I thought I'd been in control of everything. I prayed that whoever it was didn't come upstairs.

The inner door of the church opened seconds later and I heaved a sigh of relief, I managed to edge my way to look over the balcony in an attempt to discover who it was. It was dark but the shape of the figure was unmistakeable...Mulvey.

Shit, it wasn't what I was expecting, someone to have the same idea as me but at least I knew for certain what I was up against.

CHAPTER THIRTY-SIX

Like moths to a shining light we were being drawn together to meet once more...one final time. It was approaching ten thirty and the stage was almost set. Mulvey who had disappeared into the vestry almost as soon as his unexpected arrival had frightened the life out of me was sat in the back pew resplendent in his mourning suit not looking out of place at the sombre occasion. I wondered what thoughts were reverberating through his mind; surely he was more nervous than he looked. Mary and Jessie were there too, both sat in the front pew, both looking more than a little agitated. I gripped the knife in my jacket pocket tightly as the church organ suddenly sprang into life, its desolate resonance adding to the feeling of impending doom, the impending doom that only a few of us knew about.

The congregation was scattered sparsely around the church and I guessed there were fewer than twenty people all told...all about to witness a truly gruesome act.

I watched from my secret hiding place as Dean's coffin was carried into the church, a single floral tribute placed upon its lid. Tom walked a few paces behind. He was wearing the right clothes, white shirt, black tie but he still managed to look unkempt, an air of contempt seemed to emanate from him as if the whole ordeal was something of a chore, hurry up and get it over with so I can go home. Little did he suspect that it soon truly would be over but there was no way he was going home.

I kept my eye on Mulvey as the procession passed where he sat but he didn't move, he didn't even seem to pass it a second glance. Slowly the coffin and Tom moved towards the altar where the vicar stood waiting, a sympathetic smile on his lips.

I started counting down the distance left to go, ten yards, nine, eight, seven, six.... Suddenly the church door burst open and Mikey crashed into view.

Shit! What had I been doing, I should have been down there but instead I'd been transfixed by the scene, a scene that I should have been part of. I rushed down the stairs as I heard Mikey shout out a single word.

"Bastard!"

I was in a panic, I was going to be too late...I should have done it before Tom had even got into the church...someone else was going to steal my thunder.

The door was still open and I rushed in to witness what I thought was going to be Tom's death. Thankfully nothing had happened, the whole world seemed to have frozen, the whole place a deathly quiet.

Out of the corner of my eye I saw Mulvey begin to make a move and he at once became my first target. I lunged towards him shouting but I was too late, everything happened too fast. I didn't see it but Jessie must have and I heard her high pitched scream of 'Mikey!' a split second before the gun he was holding went off. I crashed into Mulvey sending him flying but my eyes were on other things, the slow motion action that was playing out in front of me, Jessie somehow in front of Tom but falling backwards almost into his arms, the sight of blood spurting from her chest as the single bullet ripped into her.

"No...o...o!" I screamed picking myself up and racing to where Jessie lay. I held her in my arms crying out her name as the final breath released itself from her body.

FADING LIGHT

ACKNOWLEDGEMENTS

Firstly a special thank you to Holly...your support and encouragement during the writing of 'Putting it Right' is something I will always remember.

A massive thank you also to Chris (Do you want another copy?) Clare and Kev, Sarah, Ali (for sales techniques) and everyone else at Nutricia.

Jordan and Sophie for putting up with my disappearing to 'the loft.'

Mum, Steve and everyone at the Parish, Deb and Robin, Jessica (sorry about the teddy!) Daniel and not forgetting the memory of Dad.

ISBN 141207599-8

9 781412 075992